THE
HAND-ME-DOWN
KID

Francine Pascal

A YEARLING BOOK

Published by
Dell Publishing Co., Inc.
1 Dag Hammarskjold Plaza
New York, New York 10017

The Author wishes to thank Linda Zuckerman
for her insightful and sensitive editing,
and John Pascal for everything else.

Copyright © Francine Pascal, 1980

Yearling ® TM 913705, Dell Publishing Co., Inc.

ISBN: 0-440-43449-1

Reprinted by arrangement with The Viking Press
Printed in the United States of America
Second Dell printing—February 1982

CW

To my daughter Susan—
the original Hand-Me-Down Kid.

ONE

"Absolutely and definitely no! You must be off your nut to think that I would ever in a million years let you put your grubby little fingers even *near* my gorgeous new cashmere sweater! You really are a little jerk, you creep. Now get out of my room and don't come back without knocking. Ever! And close that door behind you!"

That was my sister Elizabeth talking to me. She thinks she probably won't lend me her sweater today. People are always saying, so what, it won't kill you to ask, but with Elizabeth sometimes I'm not so sure.

"Ari?" Elizabeth pops her head out her room a few minutes later. This time she's using a whole new voice like she just met me. "What are you doing?"

"Nothing."

"Want to do me a favor, Ari?" It sounds almost like singing.

"I guess so."

"What's that supposed to mean?" She's back to normal. "If you don't want to do me a simple little favor just say so."

Elizabeth is a whole lot older than me. She's sixteen and I'm only eleven and even though I've known her all my life I'm still always making mistakes with her and then she's always getting angry with me. Like now, it's okay if she doesn't want to lend me her sweater, but if I don't jump at the chance to do her a favor, she's mad.

"I said I would," I tell her.

"Big deal, aren't you wonderful. Why don't you just forget it."

"Hey, no. I want to do it. I swear!" I don't understand how this happens but I always end up begging her to let *me* do *her* a favor. I suppose it looks dumb but I just don't want to be mean like she is.

"You've got to do it right now or forget it, I'll do it myself."

"I'm ready to go right this second."

"Well . . . okay . . ." she says, and then she kind of looks at me as though she's waiting for me to say thank you. I don't, so then she shrugs like I'm really ungrateful and tells me that I've got to run down to the basement and check to see that she double-locked the chain on her new bicycle. She's too much with that bike. It's a Peugeot, which is a really expensive ten-speed bike that she just got for her sweet sixteen birthday. I'm surprised she's even letting me touch the locks. That's the closest she's let me come to her precious bike since she got it almost a month ago.

"Now," and she starts giving me instructions that sound like she's talking about a baby, not just a bike. "First thing you make sure Hank's bike"—he's a kid who lives one floor below us—"isn't leaning on mine, then check that both locks are closed and see that the cover is on right."

Did you know they made covers for bikes? I didn't until Liz got one.

She's so crazy when it comes to her bike she cried for almost an hour when my dad said she couldn't keep it in the house. He said he didn't care if she wanted to keep it in her room but she isn't *that* crazy. She wanted to keep it in the front hall and he said no, everyone would be tripping on it, so then she thought maybe we could find a place in my room. I said I guess it'd be okay but my dad said it was out of the question and he wouldn't permit it no matter what I said, which was good because I really didn't want it in my room but I didn't have the guts to tell her no. Especially since that was the first nice thing she said to me all week.

Liz was really upset because she said it was dirty down in the basement and the bike would get all scratched up and then she was afraid it would get stolen. But my father said he would get her these special locks and if she was careful about remembering to lock it nobody could steal it. And then my mother said she'd get some kind of cover to protect it. Liz still kept crying and they still kept saying no and it was really strange because she hardly ever cries and when she does she usually gets what she wants. In fact, it looks to me like Elizabeth Jacobs gets exactly what she wants. I think everyone's afraid to say no to her.

I know I am.

Besides, my parents know that if they need someone to say no to they always have me.

We live on the third floor of this apartment house in Greenwich Village. That's in New York City. It's a small apartment house, only eight floors and very old, but everybody in it really loves it. Bill and Wally— they're the two old handymen—they're always polishing the brass and sweeping the floors. There's an old brass fire hydrant outside that's so shiny you can see your face in it.

Our apartment is pretty big. It's got enough rooms so that each of us kids—my sister Elizabeth, my brother Neddy (he's fourteen, and I hate him completely), and I—get to have our own rooms. Naturally my parents have theirs. Then we have a big living room, dining room, kitchen, and this little room off the kitchen that used to be a maid's room but now we use it for TV.

Even though my room is bigger than Elizabeth's, still hers is a lot prettier and nicer. It's a lot like Elizabeth. I mean she looks like she belongs there. My sister is beautiful, at least I think so. She's tall and her figure is just right and her hair is long and blond except I know it isn't as blond as it looks because she uses that shampoo stuff that makes it lighter, but I would never tell anyone. Unless she was really mean to me. Meaner than usual, anyway. Another nice thing about Elizabeth is her skin—it's very white and she never has pimples or even freckles like me. I don't have pimples either. With all my freckles there wouldn't be enough room.

Even though we're sisters we don't look at all alike. My hair is brown. My mother calls it half blond but it looks like regular brown to me, and my eyes are brown too except they're really tan, and I think they're okay because no one else I know has tan eyes. Unless maybe it's weird to have tan eyes. I hope it isn't.

I would like to look like Elizabeth when I grow up but I don't think I ever will even if I use that shampoo stuff and get all blond. I look more like my brother Neddy except his hair is a redder brown and he has twice as many freckles, which sounds impossible except it isn't because a lot of his freckles run into other freckles and then they are freckles on top of freckles, and they're all over his arms and legs and his back and everywhere. There's a girl in his class, Alice, who actually likes him. She calls him on the phone all the time. She must be a real creep to have a crush on Neddy. It's not that he's so ugly, but all he ever thinks about is his music. Either he's practicing his flute or he's got his earphones on listening to jazz. He's the most boring person I know when he isn't being mean. I don't know who's meaner, Neddy or Liz. I suppose Liz, because she's mean to Neddy too, sometimes. The oldest kids are always the meanest.

Like now. Sending me down to check on her bike is really a mean thing to do because she knows I don't like going down there alone. It's dark and sort of scary around the storage room. That's where everyone keeps their bikes and carriages and things.

I'm lucky because when I get down there to check the locks on Elizabeth's bike Mrs. Milano from the eighth floor is just coming back with her bike so I'm not going to be alone. I check the locks and they're fine and then I pull the cover back enough to get on it. Elizabeth would scream if she knew I actually sat on her precious bike.

Mrs. Milano asks me all about the bike and I can see she's impressed. I can also see that she thinks that it's mine and I let her. There's no way in the whole world that my parents would ever buy me a bike like this—they're always saying I'm too careless with everything I own—but it feels great just having someone think I own it.

"I worry a lot that someone's going to steal it out of here," I say, because I think that's what someone who really owned it would say. Liz does all the time.

"I don't want to scare you," says Mrs. Milano, "but my son's bike was stolen right out of this room last year."

"No kidding?" Liz would faint if she knew that.

"But of course he didn't have it locked up like that."

"My father says they'd have to take the whole pole if they wanted to get the bike." I think he's right too because the locks are gigantic and they wrap around this pole that's part of the building.

"Probably," Mrs. Milano says, smiling. "Just remember to keep it locked tight, Ari."

"Right," I say, and check it one last time. "See you," and I'm off upstairs.

When I get in my house Liz is in her bedroom on the

phone. That's the other terrific thing she got for her birthday—an extension in her own room. First thing I do is knock on her door.

"What!" She always sounds angry when she's talking to me, except I know she isn't now because I just did her a favor.

"The bike's okay," I tell her through the door.

"Thanks."

I push the door open just a crack. "I saw Mrs. Milano down there . . ." I start to say what happened to her son's bike but she excuses herself—her way.

"Big deal!" she snarls. "Ari, don't you see I'm on the phone? Get out! And close my door!"

I hope they steal her stupid bike. And her phone too. With her on it. Sometimes she's so mean I really hate her. Except that once in a big while she can be absolutely terrific. Sometimes when she's really miserable and unhappy and all her friends are away and there's nobody else home she'll just sit and talk to me and those are the best times of my life.

I know we could be very close if she would just give me a chance. Like with her room. I love it when she asks me to come into her room. Funny, it's part of my own house but I hardly ever get to go in there so when I do it all feels strange. I could do it when she's not home but I get worried she'll walk in and then she'd have my head. Sometimes I do it anyway. And then I go all the way—I mean, looking through her drawers, her night table, her bookcase, and all the really secret places that I discovered ages ago. Boy, she'd kill me if she knew.

One time I almost blew the whole thing. She was running around the house complaining that someone (me, of course) borrowed her green sweater and then she even accused me of lending it to someone, or better yet, trading it. It was awful the way she was making such a big thing about a lousy raggy old sweater that she's had for a hundred years—especially since I'd seen it in her drawer just that afternoon. She was even getting my mother in on it too so, without even really thinking, I said, "Why don't you look in your drawers before you start yelling at everyone?"

"I did look in my drawers, creep," she snapped back at me in that really gross fancy voice, which was mean because I was only trying to help. You see? No matter what I say she's always acting snotty to me. Anyway, without thinking, I said, "Well, if you looked in your middle drawer behind your work shirt you might find it. But of course I'm only a creep, so how would I know?"

That was dumb, because she found the sweater right where I said and then she wanted to know how come I knew exactly where it was.

I lied and said Mommy told me to put her laundry away and that's when I saw it.

"Don't do me any favors. I'll put my own laundry away. *AND STAY OUT OF MY ROOM!*"

"Drop dead!" I said, and she looked at me like I was vomit and walked away.

My mother has a fit when we tell each other to drop dead. She's superstitious or something. "Take it back," she always says, and then we have to pretend to take it back and then she says don't ever, *ever* say that again. Then she knocks on wood.

We say it all the time anyway. And sometines I think,

What if my mother's right and what if I said it to Liz and something happened and she really did die? It makes my stomach turn upside down just thinking about it. My only sister. I can't even imagine what it would be like without her. I would miss her so much, and I would feel so alone. I'd be the only daughter. Nobody but me.

I suppose we'd have to go through all her things and empty out her room—wouldn't that be horrendous? What do you do with all the things somebody owned after they're gone? I guess you just give them away to poor people. It would be dumb to give away perfectly new stuff like her suede jacket or her new bike, though. With a heavy sweater underneath I could fit into the jacket easily and I already know the combination on the bike locks.

And there are a lot of other things I wouldn't want them to give away, in fact I'd definitely want to go through everything. After all she *was* my sister and I think that everything that was hers should go to me first. Including her room.

I love her room. It's so fluffy and delicate-looking. The walls and the floors and all the furniture are shiny white, and the curtains and the bedspread and the chair are covered with little light green flowers, sort of Granny Smith apple green, and in the middle of every flower is the tiniest dot of peach. It's really a beautiful room, and everything is always perfect. I think it's weird to be so neat. Still, I would probably want to move in, and then I would want to keep most of her furniture. I hate mine. It's so baby-looking you'd throw up if you saw it. Like my chair. It's so gross I think it looks better with my clothes thrown all over it. And you wouldn't make your bed either if you had such a dumb-looking bedspread. It's ugly red (my mother says raspberry because she thinks that makes it sound better) with yellow and white cut-out dolls all over it. Ugh. Sometimes my mother has such gross taste you wouldn't believe it.

She'd probably go off the deep end if anything happened to Elizabeth because Liz is really her pet except Liz is always saying I am because I'm the baby, but she's wrong, you can tell. I'm not saying my mother doesn't like me, but it seems like she's always taking Liz's side against me. Lately I've been thinking a lot about being adopted. Like maybe I am.

Except why would anyone want to adopt another kid when they already have two? The only reason I can think of is so they have someplace right in their own family to dump all the used things . . . the hand-me-downs.

I know that skates and skis and things like that cost a lot of money and it would be dumb to just throw them out after Elizabeth and Neddy outgrow them, especially since eventually they're going to fit me perfectly. Still . . . I think I would have really liked white figure skates a lot more than Neddy's black speed skates. With the skis it doesn't make any difference anyway, we never go any more. When I was little it seemed like we used to go all the time. My parents went nuts over skiing. Everybody had to have all kinds of ski outfits and lessons and everything. Except me, of course—I was too little. The year I got big enough to get my own skis we just stopped going. I guess they lost interest.

That happens a lot. It's like everything's all used up just when I'm big enough to get in on it. Same thing with the circus. They used to take Elizabeth every single year when she was little. It was as if something horrendous would happen if she missed even one year. And then Neddy went too when he was old enough, not as much as Elizabeth but a lot. I only went to the circus three times in my whole life and the last time it was with my friend Rhona and her aunt, so that doesn't really count.

I know it's not the worst thing in the world, but I haven't had a brand-new pea jacket or rain boots or raincoat since before I can remember and even my whole bedroom is all hand-me-down from Elizabeth. Why can't I be the first to get something sometimes?

And while I'm at it, there's another thing that really upsets me. I wanted to go to tennis camp this summer but my parents said no. You know why? Because Liz went three summers ago and it didn't work out so they said it was a waste of money. I told my father that just 'cause it didn't work out for Liz doesn't mean it's not going to work out for me. That happens a lot. When I want to do something they'll say no because when Liz did it it was a mess or "last time we took Neddy the lines were so long we swore we'd never do it again." Or my father will talk about how he learned his lesson and he's not going to make the same mistake three times. It looks like they learned all their lessons way before me, and now I'm never going to get my chance for mistakes.

You wouldn't think I was exaggerating about the

adoption thing if you saw our family photo albums. Right in the beginning there's a picture of Elizabeth when they brought her home from the hospital. Then there's her first bath, the first time she lifted her head, Elizabeth drinking her milk, sleeping, crying, smiling, spitting up, and on and on. . . . Then after about a hundred pages of Elizabeth doing all these amazing things there's another fifty pages of Neddy sleeping, crying, smiling, and burping. Then there's a picture of Neddy when he was three years old holding a baby. You can't see the baby's face but everyone says it has to be me. There's a few more pictures of me here and there. One is when I'm about three at Elizabeth's eighth birthday party and then there's a school picture and some family pictures and that's all until Elizabeth's sweet sixteen. After that the camera broke. It's awful to be the littlest in the family. By the time you come along everyone is bored stiff with babies and everything's been done already.

I'm in my room when the telephone rings.

"Ari!" That's Elizabeth screaming.

What a nice picture that would make for the album.

"I hear you," I call back and run to the kitchen phone. I hope it's Rhona. She's my new best friend except I'm not sure if I'm hers.

"Hello?" I say.

"Ari?" It's Rhona. Great!

"Yeah."

"Meet me at the little park in ten minutes."

"Sure."

Click. Rhona is one of those people who never says

good-bye. She's always very busy so she doesn't have time for little things like "good-bye" or "thank you" or "please." I know my parents don't like her so much, but I think she's the most terrific person in my whole class. Maybe even in my whole school. She just got voted the class president and nobody voted against her. Not even the boys. That's probably because they're afraid to. You know what? My friend Rhona can beat up any boy in the whole sixth grade. She's very strong and she's a whole head bigger than Lewis Solarz and he's the tallest boy. A lot of the kids don't think she's so pretty because her red hair is sort of stringy and it's cut short like a boy's (not that they would ever dare to say it to her). She's got total railroad track braces and likes to wear those little round steel-rimmed glasses. When she takes those glasses off . . . watch out!

I think the best part about Rhona is that she always does exactly what she wants. She's a genius in school so the teachers all stay clear of her, and at home she has no brothers and sisters to push her around or tell her what to do. Her mother's an artist (I don't know where her father is—I never heard her ever say anything about him), and she's usually real busy so she doesn't have much time to spend with Rhona. Rhona's always saying how she doesn't like people hanging over her all the time and how she likes to be by herself. She's lucky she feels that way, because mostly her mother is out so she gets to be alone a lot. I wouldn't like that so much. I think I'd even take Neddy over being alone like she is.

Funny thing about Rhona is how she's so interested in my family. She's always asking me questions about what kind of things I do with my sister and brother and then she wants to know about what we do at family dinners and all that sort of stuff. She acts like she thinks it's all pretty dumb. Still, if it was anyone but Rhona I would think maybe she was a little jealous.

You should see Rhona's apartment. It's gigantic. It was once a loft and they had it changed into an apartment and it's big and open and sunny. When Mrs. Finkelstein is home she always has a million friends over and they just hang out. Sometimes some of them sleep over but they never bother us. In fact, they hardly even talk to us, so Rhona's on her own even when there's lots of people around. I wouldn't ever say anything to her but it's a little like nobody cares so much about her. Her mother isn't like my mother at all.

Rhona doesn't even have a real curfew at night. One time we were supposed to have a sleep-over at my house, but she changed her mind at eleven o'clock at night (she does things like that) and decided to go home. She was going to walk home by herself but my father said no, he would take her home. You should have seen her face. She's not used to anyone saying no to her, and she gave him a look that I thought would make him disintegrate. But he said there was no way he was going to allow an eleven-year-old girl to walk home alone at that hour and so he took her. Later on he said he didn't have to bother because no mugger in his right mind would tangle with Rhona Finkelstein.

I change into jeans because Rhona doesn't like shorts. I think she has red hair on her legs but I don't really know because even though we've had a lot of sleep-overs she's always very careful and nobody gets to see her legs.

The little park where I said I'd meet her is four blocks from my house, and I run the last two blocks because Rhona doesn't like it when you're late.

But I guess I'm a little late anyway because there she is standing there with two other girls, waiting for me, tapping her foot. Oh, boy, I'm in trouble.

"About time," she snaps at me. "You know I hate to be kept waiting." She's not really big into "hellos" either.

"Sorry," I say. "I ran all the way." I pant a little so she can tell I've been running.

"You call two blocks all the way?"

How did she know that? You can never fool Rhona Finkelstein.

"They're pretty long blocks."

"You can never fool Rhona Finkelstein." See, I told you. "So, kid, don't even try."

"What's up, Rhona?"

"Serafina," Rhona corrects me.

"Serafina." She changes her name all the time. She says that we were all alive before we were alive now and that we have to find out who we were then so we can know who we are now. It's called reincarnation and Rhona says there are a lot of people she knows from when she used to be someone else, and she's always telling me who everybody was. She even knew me before I was me but she says she's not ready to tell me who I was yet.

Did you know that Rhona was a queen once? Queen

Serafina. Another time she was a movie star named Theda Bara. She says she's been all kinds of people—a lot of them I'd heard about, like Joan of Arc and Michelangelo. And even when she wasn't so famous herself she was right up there. Like when she was the Ancient Mariner's cousin or when she lived two houses away from Plato and she still knows French from when she went to school with Napoleon. She sat next to him because it was size places and he was so short that he had to sit with the girls. She said that the reason he always hides his left hand is because he bit his nails. I'm not sure if I believe everything she says but I would never tell her that.

"I've decided to enter the bike marathon in Central Park," she announces. "The semifinals are tomorrow."

"That's terrific," I say.

And her two cronies, Tracy George and Margot Uptain, shake their heads and fall all over each other repeating what Rhona just said.

"And I'm going to represent our school."

"Wow, that's really terrific." I get so nervous when I talk to Rhona that a lot of the time I say dumb things or just repeat myself. I'm always trying so hard to look good so she'll like me. That's very important to me. Because the fact is that I don't have an awful lot of friends. I don't think I know how to make friends too well.

"And she's going to wear the school colors," Tracy George says, "and I'm going to lend her my new red-and-white jacket." Tracy is tall, almost as tall as Rhona, and has red hair too, except it's kinky. She's not exactly ugly, but close enough.

"And she's using my white pants," Margot chimes in, "and Matthew Young is lending her his baseball cap and he just only got it two days ago and he hasn't even worn it."

I don't know Margot too well but I like her. She's a tiny little thing with straight, flat yellow hair that hangs down to her waist. Her nose is slightly pug, like mine. I wish I could become better friends with her. And I wish I knew what they're all up to. Something's fishy, but all I do is smile and say, "That's terrific," for the third time.

"Now all I need is a bike," says Rhona, and she stares right into my eyes.

"Where are you going to get one?" I ask, and nobody says anything. Then I realize maybe she wants to borrow my bike so I say, "You can use my bike if you want but it's only a three-speeder."

My bike is a million years old. Naturally it's hand-me-down. Elizabeth got it when she was nine and then Neddy used it for a long time so now it's really beat up. Besides, it's not really fast. I don't know why she would want to use such a junky bike.

"She's got to be kiddin'," Rhona says to her friends, and then she looks at me very disgusted and says, "Stick it, friend—if that's all you're going to do for your school you can forget it."

"But that's the only bike I have, Rhona."

"Sure, kid, and that new ten-speed Peugeot Tracy George saw you riding the other day was just a mirage. Right, Tracy?"

"I must have been dreaming," Tracy says, like somebody rehearsed her.

"You mean last Saturday afternoon?" I ask Tracy, and she says yeah, and then I tell them how that wasn't my bike, it was my sister's, and the only reason she let me ride it that once was because my father said she had to because eventually it was going to be mine someday and he said I had a right to try it out. "That's the first hand-me-down thing I won't mind," I say, smiling, trying to make Rhona not look so angry.

"Borrow it," Rhona says, and it sounds like an order.

Elizabeth would never let me use her bike myself and absolutely never in a million years let me lend it to someone else. She'd probably kill me just for asking but I don't want them to know that I can't even borrow something from my own sister, so I say, "I would, but she's probably going to be using it herself."

"All Rhona needs it for is Saturday morning," Margot says. "Your sister could have it back before eleven."

"Are you sure?" I ask.

Rhona gets in front of Margot and pushes her face right up to mine. She looks angry like I insulted her.

"You think we're liars?"

"No, Rhona, I swear I didn't. I just wanted to be sure because she's going to need it for something special at eleven."

"If I say she'll have it, she'll have it."

Now Tracy gets annoyed. "The qualifying race is only from nine to ten, you know. It's no big deal to have it back by ten-thirty."

"That would really be great if you could."

"We'll try," Rhona says in a sort of nice way—for

her—and I can tell she really wants to use that bike and she would probably think I was pretty okay if I could get it for her. "What do you say, kid?"

Maybe I could. Elizabeth has guitar practice Saturday morning, and most of the time she doesn't get back until at least twelve and never before eleven. She's part of this little band, and she would never miss a session, especially since her boyfriend plays too. It wouldn't even hardly be taking a chance. She'd never know because I'd have it back before she got home.

"Sure," I say, but I can feel my stomach sliding down to my knees.

"Okay, see you right here at eight-thirty tomorrow morning," Rhona says, "and don't be late." And she's off with her two sidekicks. Nobody says good-bye.

I don't know why I'm so scared. It's really easy. Elizabeth doesn't even sleep home Friday nights because she sleeps at her friend Jill's house so they can walk over to the practice together. I guess the scary part is doing something so sneaky except that it's so hard to say no to Rhona, and besides, any other sister would lend her bike for a special race and anyway it's only going to be for an hour. And it's not like it's for something bad. It's for school, so that makes it okay. I think.

I wish I hadn't been home when Rhona called.

It's too late now. I would never not show up tomorrow. Not with Rhona waiting anyway. Nobody doesn't show up when Rhona Finkelstein's waiting.

TWO

My parents want to know why I'm so quiet at dinner. I didn't even know I was being quiet but I guess it's because even though I know it's going to be okay—about tomorrow I mean—I can't stop worrying about what will happen if I get caught.

"Nothing's wrong," I answer with a shrug.

"Maybe she's just a dummy," Neddy butts in.

"I am not," I snap, and then my mother says, "Neddy, don't start with her."

"Here comes Niagara Falls," says Neddy. He always has to have the last word.

I wasn't even near crying, but when he says that I don't know why but it makes me start. He always does that to me—teases me, I mean—and then I always cry. I hate him so much.

"Arianne, why are you crying over such a silly little thing?" my mother wants to know, and that really makes the tears come even worse.

"He's always picking on me," I say.

"Do you have to whine?" my father asks. "Can't you just speak in a normal voice?"

Now everybody's picking on me and I really can't stop crying.

"Mom?" Elizabeth says. "What am I going to wear to Lynn's sweet sixteen?"

"Your white dress with flowers?" my mother suggests.

"I can't . . . I wore that to mine," says Elizabeth, and it sounds a lot like whining to me but my father doesn't say anything to *her*.

"So?"

"So you can't wear your own sweet sixteen dress to somebody else's party," Liz says.

"Sorry, I didn't know there was a rule."

"Maaa. . . ."

Now that was *really* whining but nobody says a word. Just thinking how unfair they all are makes me start to cry again.

"What are *you* crying for now?" Elizabeth says to me, really nasty.

"I am not crying," I say, crying.

Now everybody wants to know why I'm crying, and I keep saying I'm not crying even though I am and Elizabeth says she can't eat when I make those disgusting sniffling sounds and my father asks my mother what's wrong now and my mother says she certainly doesn't know and Neddy keeps smiling at me and they're all so mean that I just get up and run out of the room.

The same thing happens all the time. Neddy teases me or Elizabeth is mean to me and then naturally I get upset and I tell my parents but they never take my side. All they care about is that I'm whining. And that makes me so unhappy I cry, and then they want to know why I'm crying all the time.

I wait for a second outside the room just to see what they'll say and all that happens is my father asks, "Why is she always crying?" And my mother says (I guess to Neddy), "This teasing will have to stop." And he claims he didn't do anything and Elizabeth says that there was this beautiful pale blue tiered skirt that would be perfect for the party and my mother wants to know how much it was and my father says he really likes that white dress with the flowers and Neddy wants to know can he have my dessert. Then I run to my room and really cry because nobody cares about me at all.

THREE

Taking the bike tomorrow morning isn't going to be a big problem. I hope. Just like I said, Elizabeth is going to sleep over at Jill's house and go straight to guitar practice from there. She left right after dinner. My parents went to the movies and there's nobody home but Neddy and me.

I'm still mad at Neddy so I'm not going to watch television because I don't want to even sit in the same room with him.

Before they left, my mother brought in my dessert and Daddy came in and talked to me about how I shouldn't pay any attention to Neddy. I told him I'll try, but I know it won't work. I can't help it. He's always saying things that make me so angry and unhappy. Sometimes I think he loves to see me crying. Almost as much as he likes to play that dumb flute except lately he's been so busy with his weight lifting he hasn't even had time to do much else. All you ever hear is him grunting and groaning, trying to lift those weights. I'm just waiting for the day he tries those big fifty-pound weights. My father says they're too heavy for him, but he doesn't listen to anyone. Besides, it's not going to work on him anyway because he's so skinny. Only thing that's going to happen is one of these days he'll lift one of those big ones and he'll just snap in half. I hope I'm home when it happens.

I've been working on my own new project. My grandma taught me how to crochet and I'm making a blanket for my bed. You just keep crocheting these little squares, and then when you have one hundred and sixty-three of them you have a beautiful blanket. So far I'm almost finished with the center of my first square. It takes a while before you get fast like my grandmother.

I'm sitting on my bed concentrating, because it's really hard to do in the beginning, when suddenly the lights go off. It's black dark because even the hall lights are out.

"Neddy! Neddy!" I call to my brother. "The lights went out!"

No answer. Probably he's got the door closed so he can't hear me. I'm not worried because we're always blowing fuses and all you have to do is push the lever in the fuse box outside the kitchen.

"Neddy!" Sometimes he gives me such a pain. I'm shouting loud so he has to hear me but he just pretends he doesn't to be mean.

"Neddy!" It's a little scary because I can't even make out my own fingers. At least not until my eyes get used to the dark.

"Neddy! Fix the fuse! Come on."

No answer.

"Neddy, you better turn those lights on or I'm going to tell!"

He still doesn't say anything.

"And besides," I shout, "I'm going to tell you were smoking two days ago in the little park, and a lot of other things . . ."

Silence.

"Wait till Mommy and Daddy come home. You just wait!"

More silence.

"Neddy?" I try to sound nice. "Just answer me, then I won't tell anything. I swear."

What if he can't? I mean, what if he didn't really turn off the lights and someone else did and whoever that someone is has Neddy locked up or something? Oh, my God!

"Neddy?"

Something squeaked. I heard it.

It sounded like the closet door in the hall. There's another sound. Like a footstep except it's a funny kind of step like something dragging.

There it is again.

It's like someone is limping. Neddy doesn't limp.

"Neddy?" I call, but all that comes out is a little squeak. No answer.

The footsteps keep coming down the hall. It's a crook, a stealer. I know it and he's already got Neddy and now

27

he's coming to steal me. I could hide in the closet or under the bed but I can't because it's like I'm frozen solid. I can't move. All I can do is listen.

Step-drag, step-drag. . . .

"Help," I cry out in a tiny whisper.

"Help!" a little louder.

Step-drag, step-drag. . . .

"Helllllllp!" In one long scream I never even knew I could do.

I'm starting on another one, even louder, when the lights go on, cutting me off right in the middle.

"What are you screaming for?" says my horrible brother, coming into my room, grinning, just as though nothing happened.

"I'm telling on you!" I scream at him.

"Crybaby," he laughs, popping the last piece of my dessert into his mouth.

"You just wait till Mommy and Daddy come home. I'm going to tell them everything you did. You're going to get punished. You just wait and see."

"No, I won't." He's so smug I could punch him except then he'd punch me back—harder.

"That's what you think."

"That's what I know."

"We'll see."

"No, we won't."

"How come?"

"Because you're not telling."

"Am too."

"I . . . don't . . . think . . . so . . ." he says in a hard, mean voice. Then he takes a step toward me and his shoulders start to hunch up and he gets a cold killer look in his eyes and I know he's going into his wolfman act.

Listen, I know it's only pretend and that he's my brother Neddy and he's really not turning into a wolfman, but when it's dark out and nobody's home and I'm all alone and his neck starts jutting out and his fingers start curling up like claws and his lip pulls back over his front teeth and he starts to snarl and growl and drop down on all fours—well, forget it, it's the most horrible scary thing you ever saw.

"Come on, Neddy, stop it . . ." I can't help it—I start begging right away.

"Grrrr . . ." he growls and starts leaping around the room. Then, as if he's seeing me for the first time, he starts to go berserk, howling and snarling and snapping at me. I jump back as far as I can into the corner of my bed, grabbing my pillow and squeezing it around my head. He rips it out of my hands and starts grabbing for my feet. I pull them away and scream, and he growls, and now I'm really hysterical, crying and screaming, and suddenly he stops dead. That's it. It's over. He's finished. I suppose the only thing left for him to do would be to eat me up.

"What are you making such a big deal about, dummy?" he says to me, shaking his head. "It's only a game."

"I don't like that game." I'm still sniffling.

"So why didn't you say so?" he asks me, like he really means it. Then he looks at his watch. "Hey, you're making me miss my program, jerko." And he shoots out of my room and back to the TV.

Maybe there really aren't such things as wolfmen,

but if there were, Neddy's mean enough to be one.

He's always doing things like that just to see if he can make me cry. He always does. I guess tonight was extra special, and I don't even really know why. Why he does it, I mean. I never do anything mean to him, and I only tell on him when he does something bad to me, and mostly I do whatever he wants me to. Like when we play games together, he's always got his own special rules, and a lot of times I know they're not fair but I never say anything. Even if I lose, I don't say anything: All I do is cry.

Way down deep inside the bottom of my heart I hate my brother.

I don't hate my sister so much except she scares me too, but in a different way. She gets mad at me for everything all the time, and then she yells at me or even worse she won't talk to me.

If she knew what I was going to do tomorrow with her bike I bet she wouldn't talk to me for the rest of my life after she finished yelling.

Lucky for me she'll never know.

I hope I hope.

FOUR

I set my alarm for six-thirty in the morning because I want to have plenty of time to get the bike out of the basement without anybody seeing me. That's not as hard as it sounds because it's really empty down there early in the morning, and besides, the door to the street is right outside the bike storage room so all I have to do is grab the bike and zip out into the street.

But first I have to get out of the apartment. That's a little hard because I hardly ever leave the house by eight o'clock on the weekend.

At seven-thirty everyone is still sleeping, so I poke my head into my parents' bedroom and whisper, "Mommy?"

I figure if I catch her fast while she's still half asleep it'll be easier.

"Shush . . ." she says and starts to get out of bed very carefully so as not to wake my father. She smiles at me, grabs her robe, and motions toward the door.

My mother's hair is tumbly curly all over her head, so she looks pretty much the same even first thing in the morning. I think she's really beautiful. And I wish I looked like her, but I don't, except our hair is the same color, but mine is stick straight. Her eyes are blue and she's what you call petite, only about five foot three. I'm five foot already and I'm only eleven. My father says I take after his side of the family and he's always telling me that it's beautiful to be tall. Last year I grew almost three inches. If I keep growing like that until I'm eighteen, I'll be seven feet tall. I'd like to see what he says then.

On the way into the kitchen I decide to tell my mother that I'm going with Rhona to a school thing, which is true except I'm leaving out the bike part.

"What school thing?" my mother wants to know.

I should have known she would.

"It's this school project"—that's a magic word for my mother. She loves school projects—"and Rhona got chosen to represent from the sixth grade down so we're all going to the park to watch her."

"Who's we?"

"Everybody. Me and Rhona and Margot and Tracy and a whole load of kids from my class. I gotta hurry because I'm supposed to meet them by a quarter after eight." That's not true but I want to get an early start because of getting the bike.

It must sound okay to my mother because she doesn't

ask me anything else about it. All she wants to know is am I going to have an egg or cereal for breakfast. If everything was normal, then I would say I wasn't hungry, which I'm not, because I'm never hungry first thing in the morning, and then she would say I had to eat something and then I'd say okay, chocolate milk, and she'd say that's not enough and we'd go back and forth like that for a while and it would usually end up with me having a bagel and cream cheese or something like that. We go through the same thing practically every morning.

"I guess I'll have a fried egg," I say.

"When are you going to learn that you have to have a proper breakfast?" my mother says, shaking her head practically before I'm finished answering.

"I said I'd have an egg."

"You did?" She looks really surprised.

"Yeah, only make sure there's no ucky stuff in it. Okay?"

"Okay," and she looks at me sort of strange and starts to fry the egg.

I'm dumb. I should have said I wasn't hungry, like always. Now she probably thinks something's fishy, and besides I'll have to eat a whole fried egg.

"Rhona said eggs make you see in the dark," I tell her so she won't think something's funny.

"I think she means carrots," says my mother with a smile.

"Maybe she said *hear* in the dark."

"That's not usually a problem."

"It could be sometimes. . . ."

"When?"

"If you were deaf?"

"Absolutely true," my mother says, "but then that would take a lot more than eggs." And she laughs and kisses me right on my nose.

I love my mommy very much but I should have asked for cereal because her eggs are really runny. Ugh.

I eat a whole lot and then I put the rest in my napkin, under my bagel, in the bottom of my juice glass, under my plate, and in the African violets.

It's only five to eight, but I'm all ready, and I think I'll go just in case my mother thinks of any other questions.

I get in the elevator and press the B button. I'm keeping my fingers crossed that I don't run into any of the joggers or that Mrs. Milano isn't going on an early-morning bike ride.

The elevator opens on the basement floor and there's no one there. Terrific.

No one's in the storage room either. I have to uncross my fingers to open the locks and take off the bike cover. I'm so nervous about someone seeing me that for the first time I'm not afraid of being alone.

It's really pretty easy. Getting the bike out the back door and up the alley behind my building. When I get past the alley gate and into the street I see the super, Mr. Rosnicof, polishing the brass moldings in front of the building. I would have to walk right past him to get to the corner but I don't want him to see me so I go in the other direction and walk all around the whole block. I don't ever look back. Somehow I always get the feeling that if you don't see someone they don't see you. I guess it's silly, but it makes me feel better.

It would be faster if I rode the bike but I would never sneak it out just for me to ride. That would really be awful. This way I feel like I'm doing it for the school and that's not half so bad. In fact, I think that's hardly bad at all.

It's not even ten after eight when I get to the little park. This year a lot of the big kids in the eighth grade helped plant pansies, and the whole park has a purple and yellow border around the edge. It's so beautiful, especially first thing in the morning before people start messing it up with papers and beer cans. Even though the flowers are pretty they don't smell flowery—don't ask me why. But the park smells great anyway. It's from the grass, I guess. They cut it yesterday. I love that smell. It's like the country. Actually the city always smells sweet and fresh in the morning like clean water. I wonder why it doesn't last all day.

There's hardly anyone in the park this early except for people like Bag Mary, and she probably sleeps there. She's one of those shopping bag ladies who live in the streets. You see a lot of them in New York and most big cities. Most of the street people drink too much but some of them, like Bag Mary, are just peculiar, sort of out of it. She's always wearing her whole wardrobe, three or four sweaters and a ratty fur coat and some wool hats, no matter how hot it is. Then she carries two shopping bags stuffed with what looks like rags but I guess it's extra shoes and things. Some of the shopping bag ladies are mean, always shouting and angry, even when there's no one around. One old lady is always arguing with invisible people. You should hear her—it's weird. Bag Mary's never angry and she has a little dog that sometimes rides in her shopping bag. I talk to Mary and she's always very nice to me. You can't exactly talk directly to her—you have to talk to Wendy, that's her dog, and then Mary answers like she's Wendy.

"Hi, Wendy," I say to the dog when I get to her bench.

"Hi," Mary says, but she doesn't look at me because I'm having a conversation with Wendy. Mary never smiles but I guess she doesn't have much to be happy about.

"That's a beautiful bike you got there, honey," Wendy says, sort of.

"Thank you," I say, "but it's not mine. . . ."

I start to tell her more, then I think that's dumb and just say thank you again.

"Well," I say, "I have to go now. I'll see you around. Bye, Wendy."

"Bye, honey."

And I pet Wendy's head. I wish I had a dog biscuit or something to give her because she really looks skinny, and I'll bet Mary hardly ever has enough money to buy her biscuits. I'm going to keep one in my pocket from now on. Just for Wendy.

It's still too early for Rhona, so I stand the bike up and sit down on the grass next to it. Then I lie back and watch the sky through the trees. When the breeze blows the leaves they look like they're silver underneath and I always get fooled and have to look harder and then I see it's just the sunshine catching the bottom of the leaves. I wonder how come that happens.

"Help! Help!" Somebody is shouting practically right behind me, and I jump up and look around.

There are two boys about fourteen or fifteen, and they're being mean to one of the old bums. They keep taking his hat and tossing it back and forth. They're much faster than he is, and besides he's got a bad limp and all he can do is stand there and call for help, except that there's no one around but me.

I don't know who the boys are, and I'm really sort of afraid to start up with them, but I hate the way they're being so awful to that poor old man, so I kind of move over a little closer, but still not too near, and I say, "Hey, you shouldn't do that."

But they don't hear me because they're shouting and laughing so hard, so I go a little nearer.

"Hey, you better stop that," I say louder. I don't want to get them mad at me, but I can't help being angry because it's such an awful thing they're doing.

Now they both stop and turn around. One of them is short and chunky with the kind of long stringy hair that people used to wear a long time ago in the sixties. His T-shirt is grungy looking and it says, "Get off my case," which is nasty like he is. The other boy isn't so awful looking because his hair is regular looking and he doesn't look so dirty. He's about Neddy's size, and the way they're teasing the old man almost reminds me of Neddy except that he would never do that to anyone but me.

"You going to make us?" the bigger one sneers at me.

"You just better stop that or you're really going to get in trouble," I say.

That breaks them up because I guess I really don't look so scary to them. Well, you know something? They don't look so scary to me either because now I'm absolutely furious. They've made the poor old man cry. It's terrible. He's putting his face in his hands and he's sobbing. I know it's strange to cry over a hat, but he looks so poor that something little like a hat probably means a whole lot to him. Maybe he can never buy another one again in his whole life. How could those rotten boys be so horrible!

But they don't care. They just keep throwing his hat back and forth, and there's no chance he could ever catch it.

But maybe I can.

I don't usually do things like this, but there's no one else around, and I'm going to cry myself if they don't stop that.

"You just stop that!" I shout at them in as grown-up a voice as I can do. Now they start yelling nasty things at me. Awful words I don't even want to repeat, and that makes me more nervous because I know they're not kidding around any more. Still, I can't stop. Even though my whole body is shaking I make a grab for the hat. But I miss and fall down, and they think that's hysterical. Now the bigger one starts throwing the hat as high as he can straight up in the air and catching it. He does it right over my head. I stand up and just watch, waiting for the right time to jump in and snatch it.

They keep calling me names, but I don't take my eyes off the hat.

Now!

A little breeze catches the hat and it starts to go straight out away from him. And I start running toward it. I'm pretty fast at running and this time I go full speed. I grab the hat just as it touches the ground and clutch it to my stomach, sitting down and bending all the way over so that no part of it is sticking out. I've got my eyes squeezed shut waiting for one of them to make a grab for it. I'm holding on as hard as I can. I'm afraid to look up because if I see them coming toward me I might get scared and let go.

Every second I think someone's going to jump on me, but nothing happens. I sneak a tiny peek out of the corner of my eye but I don't see anyone. Now I turn my head just a little more but I still stay all hunched up. Where did they go?

I get up. The boys are gone. There's only the old man and he's sprawled out on the bench. My God! They must have hit him because his head is rolled back and his eyes are closed. I hope he isn't dead. Ohhh . . . please don't let him be dead!

I really have to swallow hard and force myself to go up to him because I'm afraid of what I'll see.

His hat smells. I didn't notice before but now I see how disgusting it is and I hold it out far away from me and walk slowly up to the bench. I don't see any blood so that's good, except that I'm still shaking.

Just as I get close to him he snores. He's sleeping! I can't believe it! I don't mean to sound like I'm sorry he's not hurt but I just didn't expect him to go right to sleep after all that. I stand there waiting for him to wake up and he doesn't. He looks so peaceful you'd think he was home in his own bed. I feel like a jerk standing here with his hat in my hands. Probably if I wake him up he won't even remember what happened so I lean forward, far as I can, and drop the hat into his open lap. Oh, well, at least I got his hat back for him. I wish he was awake so I could see how happy he was about it. That would make me feel like what I did was important. Still, I think when he does wake up he'll feel good to know he has his hat.

With all this I forgot about the time and Rhona and the bike. . . .

THE BIKE!

Where is it? *My God, it's gone!*

FIVE

I start looking all over the place. I can see the whole park from where I'm standing because it's very small and flat but there's no bike. I start running toward where I left it and my heart is pounding so hard. This is the most terrible thing that ever happened to me in the whole world.

There's no trace of it. It's gone. I feel like I'm going to throw up unless I find that bike right this minute. I'm absolutely going to cry. I'm crying already. I wish I'd never even met Rhona. It's all her fault.

Rhona! Of course. That would be just like her. To take the bike, I mean, without even saying anything to me. She would just ride it away to the race. That's what happened. I know it.

Except it's not so, because here comes Rhona right now with Margot and Tracy and they're all walking. From almost half a block away I can see Rhona is getting angry. She's got her hands on her hips and she's walking real fast.

"Well? Where is it?" she says, coming right up to me. I only come up to her shoulders so I have to bend my head back just to look at her face. Way back because she's practically right up against me.

"I don't know," I say. "Somebody took it. . . ." and I start crying again. I don't like to cry in front of all of them but I can't help it.

"Yeah, sure," Rhona says, giving Margot and Tracy a look over the top of her glasses, as though she thinks I'm making the whole thing up.

"It was stolen. I swear," I say. "I brought it with me right here and then these boys were teasing this old man—" I point to where the old man was but he's gone too. "Well, he was here before. I swear. . . ."

"So now what am I supposed to do, huh?" Rhona doesn't even let me tell her the whole story. All she cares about is that she won't have a bike to ride in the race.

"Boy, thanks a lot," says Tracy. I never liked Tracy.

And then Margot rolls her eyes and everyone is really annoyed with me for letting the bike get stolen. They make me feel like it was my fault, so I say the only thing I can, "I'm sorry."

Margot and Tracy shake their heads as if they can't believe I would ever do such a thing to Rhona.

"Do me a favor, huh?" Rhona says to me.

"Anything." I tell her and I mean it. I really don't want her to be mad at me. I don't care about Margot and Tracy, but Rhona is my best friend. From my side anyway.

"Drop dead!" Rhona says, and turns around before I can say anything, and with Margot and Tracy right behind her walks away.

Even though my eyes are bulging with tears, I can still see good enough to watch them walking through the park and out the other side. Probably Rhona will never talk to me again as long as I live. And neither will my sister Liz when she finishes screaming. This is the unhappiest I've ever been since before I can remember. It's like my heart broke all over the place and slid down into the bottom of my stomach. And I'm all by myself. I don't even like being all by myself when everything is good. But now it's the worst ever. If only I hadn't promised Rhona. If only . . . if only Liz hadn't gotten that bike for her birthday none of this would have happened. They could have bought her a regular bike. None of her friends have an expensive Peugeot. She's so spoiled. My parents are always buying expensive things for her and she really doesn't deserve them. At least I don't think so. If I were Mom I would buy her a Woolworth's bike . . . and if she didn't like it I would say, "Tough." Besides, then if someone steals it it's not so horrible. And maybe if it didn't cost so much nobody would want to steal it anyway.

I hate people who steal things. They make everybody so unhappy.

Maybe I should get the police after them—I mean the

robbers who stole the bike—but I can't call the police because I wasn't supposed to have the bike in the first place. Maybe if I wait here a little longer whoever took it will feel bad and bring it back. Then they'll say they're sorry and they didn't mean to keep it anyway. They just wanted to ride it awhile because they're very poor and they would never get a chance to ride a Peugeot and I'll say all right but you shouldn't do that again because you could really get in trouble and besides you make the person who owns the bike feel awful. Especially if it's the person's sister who's not allowed to borrow it in the first place.

I wait for a long while, but I guess they're really going to keep it.

The only thing left is to go home and tell my mother what happened. I wish I could think of something else so I didn't have to tell. Maybe when I get home the stealers will have brought it back.

It could happen, you know. Even stealers can change their minds.

SIX

I'm all out of breath when I get to the basement door. I wish . . . I pray . . . please, God, make the bike be back where it should be.

I'm very quiet going through the basement to the storage room. It's pitch-black. I shut my eyes tight and turn on the light.

I swear to God and hope to die that I will never ever borrow Liz's bike again so long as I live, and I'll never even touch it or ask to ride it or ever do anything wrong again in my whole life if only that bike is back where it's supposed to be.

I open my eyes.

They didn't. Bring it back, I mean. Boy, they stink. I guess there's nothing left to do but tell my parents. Maybe they'll know what to do.

And maybe they can do it without telling Liz. Boy, she's going to kill me.

Then I think of something.

As long as the bike is gone and nobody can get it back, it's really silly to make things even worse. No matter what really happened, the bike is gone and Liz would probably feel better if she thought it just got stolen nice and simple. Remember how Mrs. Milano said they broke in and took her son's bike last year? So it could happen again.

I know where there's a lot of leftover stuff like pieces of cabinets and all that. The handymen are always throwing junk in a big pile way over in the corner behind Mr. Crowley's old refrigerator, so I go over to see if maybe there's some broken pieces of chain, then I can make it look like the stealers broke Liz's chain when they took the bike.

I'm going to do it, you know.

I'm going to make it look like somebody broke in and stole the bike. I've already decided. It's terrible, isn't it? It's an even bigger lie than sneaking the bike out in the first place, but I'm scared of what will happen if they find out the truth. Besides, if it's gone, it's gone, and what difference does it make how it really went? Anyway, if it does make a difference it's mostly to me, and I'm really sorry already so what good will it do if they know the truth? Maybe I'll tell them later, like when I'm old and going to get married or sometime like that. But not now. Absolutely not now.

I guess I'm just lucky because there's a perfect piece of chain that looks a lot like the one Liz had. I take the broken chain over and wrap it partway around the pole so it looks like someone broke the locks off. I put Liz's good chain way under the pile of junk in the corner. It's like in the movies when the murderer is trying to cover his tracks. Maybe I should wipe my fingerprints off the chain.

That's probably silly so I only do it a little bit with the bottom of my T-shirt. I'm doing everything as fast as I can and trying to remember if I forgot anything. I look around to make sure I didn't leave something like a handkerchief with my initials on it on the floor. I guess it couldn't happen because I don't have those kind of hankies. Still, I want to be sure because that's how they always catch people on TV.

Instead of going up the elevator from the basement I go out the side door and walk around and come in through the front lobby the way I always do. The doorman, Everett, just nods to me. It's the wrong time of the year for him. The only thing he ever talks to me about is the weather. In the summer he always says, "Hot enough for you?" and in the winter, "Cold enough for you?" In the spring and the fall all he does is nod.

I don't meet anyone in the elevator, and, lucky me, I remembered my key so all I do is slip into my house quietly and go right into my room as though I've been there for hours.

It's very quiet in the house. My parents must be out playing tennis, and Neddy's got his softball game Saturday mornings. Liz probably isn't back from her rehearsal yet.

She'll probably spend the whole day with Eddie Gonzalez—that's her boyfriend—so maybe she won't even know about the bike. And then my mother said it might rain tomorrow so she won't use it then. And Monday is school so she could go for a long time without even knowing it's missing.

So maybe I don't have to start worrying for at least two days, and by then maybe I could find it. I could start looking this afternoon.

I start into the kitchen but I suddenly hear some giggling coming from Liz's room. I tiptoe up to her room. She's got the kind of door that folds back so you can see a lot through the crack in the middle.

I peek in. Liz is there with Eddie, and they're fooling around on the bed. I can't see everything, but it looks like they're wrestling, except I'm not that dumb. They're making out. They always do as soon as my parents go out. I hate to be home with them because all they ever do is go into the bedroom and close the door. I don't know how come they don't get tired of doing the same thing all the time. I would get tired of kissing and hugging for hours. I wouldn't even like it so much for minutes even though Eddie is really cute looking. He's got very dark hair and tannish skin that looks sunburned except it's not. He's Puerto Rican. There are hardly any Puerto Rican kids in our school because it's a private school and it costs a lot of money but they do give scholarships to poor kids if they're really smart. Eddie is a brain, especially in math, and his family is very poor. He's the oldest, and he's got three brothers and two sisters, and his mother is going to have another baby in the fall. They must really love kids a whole lot to have so many.

My parents say that the Gonzalezes live in a bad neighborhood and they don't allow Liz to go there. They say it's okay if Eddie comes to our house but she can't go to his. She goes there sometimes anyway, but they don't know. Sometimes my parents are super protective. They wouldn't like it much if they knew she and Eddie were hanging out in her room either.

I'm just backing away when the front door opens and slams shut. That's got to be Neddy. I go straight into the kitchen so he won't catch me spying on them.

"Anybody home?" he yells from the front hall.

"Yeah," I call, and at the same time Liz shouts out not to come in her room.

"Liz?" Neddy sounds surprised. He goes right to her door and shoves it open. I would never do that.

"I told you not to come in," she says, and she's very angry. I kind of drift over to the doorway because I love to see them shout at each other instead of me.

Neddy doesn't pay any attention to how mad she is. He asks, "What are you doing home?"

She snaps at him, "What does it look like I'm doing?" Eddie stays out of the whole thing.

"I thought you were out with your bike," I hear him say from the kitchen.

Uh oh . . .

"What are you talking about?" she says. "I didn't touch my bike today."

"Well," Neddy asks, "who's got it?" Right away Liz starts screaming, and she doesn't even know anything yet. By now I've come out of the kitchen and I'm right behind Neddy.

"No one has it!" She gets hysterical so fast. "It's

49

down in the basement. Isn't it? Are you saying that it's not there? Where is my bike!"

"I don't know," Neddy says, and he turns to me and rolls his eyes like she's crazy.

Now she grabs Eddie and rushes out of the apartment, wailing, "My bike . . . my bike."

Naturally we run out after her.

I would like not to but it would be funny if I didn't.

It's very embarrassing riding down the elevator with Liz because she's moaning and crying as though somebody died. Bet she wouldn't make so much of a fuss if I got stolen.

The minute the elevator door opens she jumps out and races through the corridor toward the storage room. Neddy and I are a few feet behind her. Suddenly there's this horrible shriek. Oh, I wish I were dead.

Mr. Rosnicof, the super, comes rushing out of the boiler room with a half of sandwich in his hand and shouting, "What's the matter? What happened? Who's hurt?" He practically runs into us.

I forgot about Mr. Rosnicof being outside when I took the bike. I hope so hard he didn't see me with it.

"Ohhh, Mr. Rosnicof, they've taken my bike . . ." Liz says, throwing herself into the super's arms, sobbing.

Mr. Rosnicof pulls back a little because I think he doesn't want to get Liz's tears all over his shirt. Mr. Rosnicof never looks like a super even when he's working. I mean his clothes are always so neat and clean, and his hair is combed shiny down flat, and he's got a big black mustache that he makes pointed at the ends.

My mother says he thinks he's a movie star. My father says that the reason he never looks like he's working is that he never is. The tenants in the building are always complaining about Mr. Rosnicof and he's always complaining about them. But he's nice to us kids so I like him okay.

"Take it easy now, Elizabeth," says Mr. Rosnicof. "We'll find it." And he looks at me, and I can't tell whether he knows or whether he's just plain looking. I don't say anything and try to look as normal as I can, even though I'm starting to shake all over. "Maybe somebody borrowed it," he says.

I hold my breath, waiting for him to point to me. Liz shakes her head no, she didn't lend it to anyone.

"Then maybe," he says, "someone moved it to another place. Let's have a look."

Whew! I'm safe. He didn't see me.

And we all follow Mr. Rosnicof into the storage room. He pulls a flashlight out of his back pants pocket and shines it all around the room.

I don't know why I'm looking, I already know it isn't there. Meanwhile Neddy goes over to where the bike is supposed to be and out of the corner of my eye I can see him bending down and picking something up.

"Hey, look here," Neddy says. He holds up the broken chain. Liz and Eddie and Mr. Rosnicof hurry over to look. I sort of hang behind them a little way. Now I'm worried. Suppose she knows it isn't hers?

"Oh, what a shame," Mr. Rosnicof says, shaking his head and taking the piece of chain from Neddy. "Looks like somebody used a hacksaw on this thing."

"They've stolen my bike!" Now Liz is crying into Eddie's shoulder, and he's telling her it's going to be all right. I don't know how, though.

"How about it, Mr. Rosnicof?" Neddy asks. "Do you think we should call the cops?"

"Absolutely," he says. "But let me check around and see if that's the only thing missing." And he looks carefully all around the room. "Hey," he says, pointing to an empty corner, "I think they took another bike."

"I don't think so," I say, and they all look at me and all of a sudden I get hot all over, ". . . because there wasn't ever anything in that corner."

"How would you know?" Neddy says, being awful.

"I know because Mrs. Weyland used to keep her old baby carriage there. Remember?"

Everybody says yeah, but I don't think anybody remembers because I just made it up. I guess it sounds right, thank God.

We all follow Mr. Rosnicof into his little office. It's not really a regular office. It's more like his workroom, with all kinds of tools hanging on the wall and a cot in the corner where everybody says he's always sleeping when anything important goes wrong. The tenants say that all he does is hang around outside the building so he can watch the girls walk by. He looks much too old to me for caring about pretty girls. I think he must be even older than my father.

We sit around for about fifteen minutes, waiting for the police, and everybody's trying to guess what happened to the bike. Even me, because it would look funny if I didn't. Then I make a mistake and tell them how Mrs. Milano's son's bike was stolen just last year. Liz asks how come if I knew that I didn't tell her, and she's beginning to make me feel it was my fault that the bike was stolen, which is weird because it really is my fault, but not the way she thinks. You see how Liz always blames me for everything? So what if she's right this time? It's for the wrong reasons, so it doesn't count.

"That's no fair," I tell her. "I tried to tell you but you were too busy talking on the phone."

"Since when are you so polite that you don't butt right into the middle of my conversation?" she says, really snotty. "Huh? Since when?" Then she does her imitation of me. "It's no fair," she says in a squeaky little voice that doesn't sound at all like me. "I tried to tell you that the house was on fire but you were talking on the phone. Gawd!" she says to Eddie. "See what I mean? She's impossible."

"Come on, Liz," Eddie says. "You can't blame Ari. Things get stolen from basements all the time. Besides, she probably did try to tell you."

"Now you're on her side too? Terrific," Liz says, and she looks like she's going to burst into tears any second, which really upsets Eddie because he's very nice and sweet. I don't know how he can like that witch.

"I'm not on anybody's side, Liz," he says, putting his arm around her and hugging her. "I just don't think you should blame Ari."

I wish he was my brother. I'd trade Liz and Neddy for one of him anytime.

"Did they ever find it?" Neddy asks me.

"Huh?"

"Milano's bike, dummy."

"Oh . . . I don't know." I shrug.

"How come?"

"How come they didn't find it?" Sometimes they get me so confused, and then they get angry that I don't know what they're talking about.

"No, jerko," Neddy says, rolling his eyes like I'm too dumb for words. "How come you didn't ask Mrs. Milano? She should've asked her, right, Liz?" He's always trying to get on Liz's good side.

"Right," Liz says. "Boy, Ari, sometimes you're so dense I can't believe it."

And they're going on about how I'm so dumb and they're forgetting all about how the bike is missing. All they care about is picking on me. Except Eddie, of course. Just when it looks like they'll never stop, the police come. Two really big policemen wearing clubs and guns and everything.

Mr. Rosnicof goes straight up to them, shakes their hands, and introduces himself as the superintendent only he makes it so fancy it sounds more like he's the landlord. He starts to tell them about the bike, and while they listen to him they keep watching us. Me, mostly, I think, and it's making me very nervous.

SEVEN

I think they know the bike wasn't really stolen from the basement. Just from the way they're pretending that they don't even notice me. I can tell it's phony. First thing they ask is whose bike it was. Liz tells them it was hers and then she gives them the whole story. She tells it so well that we're all really listening, like it was a TV show or something. She starts right from the beginning, how she got it for her birthday and all, and everybody goes, "Aahhh . . ." and about how she didn't want to keep it in the basement in the first place but her parents made her, and you can tell everybody is thinking, *Wow, they stink.* And then she shows how she discovered the bike was gone and she even gasps and puts her hand over her mouth and then big fat tears all gooked up with green eye shadow start rolling down her cheeks. That doesn't look so good but she really knows how to tell a story the best of anybody. My father says she's going to be a great actress one day. You can tell the police think so too, the way they try to calm her down.

"Who's he?" The big cop is pointing to Neddy.

"He's my brother," Liz tells him, and the policeman nods as if he was writing it all down in his head. He's scary looking even though he has rosy cheeks like a doll but still and all he looks really mean. His badge says "Fitzroy."

"What about her?" He's nodding at me. His eyes are burning right into my head. I told you. He knows.

"She's nobody," Liz says, "just my kid sister."

"Okay," says Fitzroy, pretending I'm not important. I think maybe he's very smart even though he doesn't look it.

Meantime the other policeman, who is even scarier looking because he looks so angry, is just standing there staring at Eddie and Eddie looks even more scared than me.

"Hey, you," he finally says, calling Eddie.

"Yes, sir," says Eddie. Boy, I never heard Eddie say "sir" to anyone before.

"How do you fit into this group? You another brother?" And he kind of chuckles as though he made a funny joke. Nobody else laughs, not even the other policeman. I think he meant it nasty because Eddie is Puerto Rican and we're not.

"What do *you* think?" Eddie says in the same kind of

tough voice as the policeman's. Liz sort of moves over closer to Eddie as if she's going to protect him.

"He's my friend," Liz says.

"Maybe," the cop says, looking very hard at Eddie. "When did you get here?"

"I don't know." Eddie shrugs. "A couple of hours ago, I guess."

"What about this morning? Where were you then?" Now even the first cop is getting into it. I don't know if I'm right but I think the reason they're picking on Eddie is because they think he stole the bike, and the reason they think that is because he's Puerto Rican. I know it sounds stupid but that's just what it looks like. That's how prejudice is—real dumb. Boy, my parents would be really angry if they saw this. Even I don't like it except that if they weren't picking on him they'd probably be picking on me. Maybe they're just doing this to throw me off the track. If only they don't know yet, then maybe I'll have enough time to find the bike myself. That's all I need, you know, just a little more time. I know I can find it.

"I was at band practice all morning and then I went home for a while," Eddie is telling them. "And then I came straight here."

"How long were you home?" the angry policeman asks. The name on his identification tag says "Jones." He's pretty fat, with gray hair and a red face that seems to keep getting redder.

"A couple of hours."

"Yeah? Who saw you?"

"I don't know. My brother, I guess."

"What's his name?"

"What do you need my brother's name for? Look, officer, I didn't steal that bike."

"This is crazy," Liz says, and she's really angry and not one bit afraid. "You have no right to talk to my friend like that."

"Right." Neddy agrees with her.

I don't say anything.

"Whoever stole that bike," Eddie says, "had to break the chain. Why would I do that? I already know the combination."

"That true, miss?" Fitzroy asks.

"Of course he does," she says. "I told you he was my friend."

"That's it then," he says to his partner. "Nothing else here." And they both turn to leave.

"Wait!" Liz squeals. "Where are you going? Aren't you even going to look for it?"

"Look, miss," Officer Fitzroy says, "there's hundreds of bikes stolen every year and almost no chance of recovering them. You got to face facts."

Now Mr. Rosnicof gets into it. "You mean you're not going to do anything? Like you're saying, 'Well, that's too bad'? What are you police for if you can't even find a kid's bike?"

"Hey, just a minute, fella," Fitzroy replies. "I didn't say we weren't going to try. All I mean is that she shouldn't build up her hopes."

"You got a city of animals out there waiting to grab anything that isn't nailed down," the awful policeman says. "What do you expect us to do?"

"Easy does it," his partner says. "They just want to know that we're trying."

Mr. Rosnicof is still angry, so he says, "Doesn't sound like you're going to be trying too hard."

"Sure we are," the nicer policeman says. "We're going right down to the station now and check out a few things. We'll let you know how it's going the minute we find anything out. How's that?"

"A lot of good that's going to do," Liz says, and she looks so sad that the nicer policeman says to her really sweetly, "We'll try our best, miss. Could you give us a description of the bike?"

"It's beautiful," she says, "the most gorgeous Peugeot you ever saw in your life."

"Could you be more specific? Like what color is it?"

"Oh, right. Well, it's sort of bluish greenish. In the sun it looks aqua but it's really not. It's got too much blue in it. It's like that ring Mommy has." She turns to me. "The one she wears on her pinkie."

I nod, and the policeman tries to rush her along. "Okay, I got that. Anything else we should look for?"

"Well, it's got this silvery white streak running down both sides that's kind of iridescent and the seat is a soft beigy fawn. Sometimes it looks like it's picking up a silvery tint from the handlebars. I've covered the hand grips in bright clean white tape that really sets off the streaks and makes the whole bike glisten."

"I got it," the cop says, reading from his notebook. "It's a blue Peugeot with a white streak and a tan seat. Right?"

"I guess so," Liz says, completely disappointed.

"Okay," he says, closing his book, and both cops leave and we all talk about how awful they were. Well, Fitzroy, the one with the rosy cheeks, wasn't so bad but the other one was horrible the way he was picking on Eddie. Everybody says they're going to go back upstairs to wait for my parents but I tell them maybe I'll go look around.

"Maybe whoever took the bike had to leave it because they had to get away fast or maybe they just changed their mind and didn't even . . ."

I stop in the middle because nobody's listening, not even Eddie. I hate it when they treat me like I wasn't even there. They do that, Liz and Neddy anyway, all the time. It's because I'm so much younger. They think I don't know what I'm talking about. They should know how much I know about this whole thing. Even if I told them, they probably wouldn't listen anyhow. I start to go out through the basement deliveryman's door but suddenly Liz wants to know where I'm going.

"I told you I was going to look for the bike."

"Oh, God," Neddy says. "There goes Nancy Drew."

I hate him.

"Shut up," I tell him, and then Liz tells me I'm not supposed to say shut up. My mother has this thing about saying shut up and now suddenly Liz is my mother, which is even worse than when she's my big sister. "Then make him stop picking on me."

"Shut up, Neddy," she says.

"You said *I* shouldn't say shut up," I tell her.

"Dummy, I'm on your side," Liz practically screams at me. She's awful even when she's supposed to be helping me. *"Now* what are you doing?" she wants to know.

"Nothing," I tell her.

"I thought you were going to look for my bike."

"I am."

"Great. So go."

Even if I found it she probably wouldn't say thank you. I go out the basement door, up the alley, and head toward the little park. Maybe I can find those awful boys. But they were so mean they probably wouldn't help me anyway. The old man should, though, because I was really nice getting his hat back for him. If he remembers.

EIGHT

On Saturday afternoons the park gets pretty busy.
Mostly it fills up with families who mainly go to the
playground area where the swings are. I never go to
that part any more. Not this year anyway. Sometimes I
wouldn't mind going on the swings or the monkey bars
but I would feel dumb, especially if anyone saw me.
They'd probably think I was a baby. Mostly the grown-
ups don't allow the park people, the drunks and shopping bag ladies, inside the playground area, so I don't
bother to look there. I walk around the outside rim
where they have the flowers and work my way into the
center of the park. A couple of times I think I see the old
man but when I get close it turns out to be someone
else. I would know his face anyplace. One time I think I

lly fast, and besides, working the mon-
tricky as it looks. Except that the rain
arder because it's really coming down
s are slippery. But she follows exactly
hen she gets it right she lets out a big
ls around a couple of more times and
feet and with a big smile on her face
lot. I always love the monkey bars,

now that I'm a beginning gymnast.
Jacobs. You're Jane, aren't you?"
ichardson."

away that I'm going to like Jane. I
uch about her. She's new in the neigh-
e's something so friendly and easygo-
t I just know we're going to get along
round as a plate, with big brown eyes
ps that turn up in a smile even when
e's really pretty except her figure is
Mine is straight up and down skinny
ght up and down chubby. She sort of
muffin.

that after you just meet someone. At
ve anything to say, so you just stand
nny, those things never seem to hap-
They always have lots to say. I guess
e trouble as I do because she just sort
ith a smile that begins to turn funny
ething about the whole thing starts to

see him and then it turns out it isn't even a man but an old woman except she has so many clothes on I almost couldn't tell.

Now I'm beginning to feel really awful. Maybe I'll never find the bike and it will always be on my conscience that I was the one who got Liz's bike stolen and I'll always feel like I'm dishonest. I hope this isn't the beginning of being a criminal. It's not funny because that's the way people start out—on a life of crime, I mean. They start doing bad things when they're little and then the things get worse and worse and bigger and bigger until they're gangsters with guns and brass knuckles and then they go to jail and all. And I'll bet most of them don't even start off with something as serious as mine. Boy, my family would be so hurt and ashamed if they knew. I can't help crying when I think about this, because it's the most horrible thing that I ever did in my whole life and there's nobody I can even tell it to.

I go completely around the park four times and I still don't see the old man or even those boys. By the time I get back to the playground area it's starting to drizzle and all the people are grabbing their kids up so fast you'd think it was boiling oil instead of only water coming down. Parents are so funny about rain. They go crazy if you even get the slightest bit wet. Like you're going to catch pneumonia instantly. I feel so unhappy I don't want to go home and as long as nobody knows where I am and it's pretty warm I decide to sit out the rain. Besides it gives me a chance to play on all the kids' stuff because now nobody's going to see me.

I start on the swings and I try to swing between the big gloppy drops but they hit me anyway. I put my head back and open my mouth and let the drops fall right into my mouth. Once, somebody said that there's a piece of dirt in every raindrop. They don't taste dirty.

The monkey bars are my favorite but they're really babyish. I can hang by my feet in my sneakers. My mother goes crazy when she sees me do it but she's not around, so I hang there awhile and it makes me feel sort of numb with a whirling zinging sound in my ears and everything topsy-turvy. I like it that way because it's all so different and maybe in this upside-down world I wouldn't have to worry about any bikes. Nobody rides bikes upside down, do they? I can do this thing where I hold onto the bars with my hands and let my head hang way down and swing my legs completely around. It looks harder than it really is.

"Hey, that's pretty good," a voice near me says. Even from my upside-down position I can see it's a girl around my age. She steps back a little, and I can see that it's Jane Richardson, the new girl in my class. She'll probably tell Rhona and I'll look like a jerk baby playing on the monkey bars.

"Hi," I say, still hanging there. Maybe she won't recognize me upside down. But how long can I stay this way? My head feels really prickly and funny.

"Hi," she says.

I'm starting to get sick to my stomach. I wish she would go away so I could get up. But she just stands there.

"Well," I say, "I'll see you around."

That makes h
"That's really g
"Huh?" I say.
blood racing to
"You know, th
"Oh."
"Would you sl
I can't tell if s
me to show her
another second c
and land neatly
of the bars to
spinning.
"That turn lool
she isn't teasing
thing?"
Wow. I never
gymnast, I meal
That's great. Fro
time and just say
those Olympic sta
"Well, I'm not
studying to be on
"That's terrific,
Olympics?"
"Probably," I s
with my legs that
of something very
about the monkey
really all the way
"Could you shov

Jane learns re
key bars isn't as
makes it a little
now and the ba
what I say and v
whoop! She whi
then drops to he
says, "Thanks
don't you?"
"Yeah," I say
"My name is An
"Right. Jane
I decide righ
don't know too
borhood but th
ing about her t
great. Her face
and pink, pink
she's talking.
worse than mi
and hers is str
reminds me of
"Hi," I say.
"Hi."
It's always I
first you don't
there staring.
pen to grownı
Jane has the s
of stands ther
on her face. S

tickle me and I let out a little giggle and then she does too and pretty soon we're both laughing and then we're hysterical and I don't even know why but it's terrific because both of us look so crazy dripping wet and hysterical.

"Come on," she says, and starts running across the park. I run after her. Every time she turns around to look at me she bursts out laughing, and so do I, and it's raining so hard we can barely see where we're going.

When we get out of the park Jane heads toward Eighth Street and I follow her. She ducks into the first store we pass and it turns out to be a fancy underwear shop. They're not so happy to see us because we're dripping all over their floor.

"What can we do to help you young ladies?" the lady behind the counter says with one of those squeezed-out smiles where you know the only way she wants to help you is right out the store.

"Well," Jane pulls herself together and says in the fanciest voice you ever heard, "my companion and I are interested in lingerie."

"Just what type of lingerie are you interested in?"

"Brassiere type."

"For yourself?"

"Right," Jane says, and looks sort of insulted.

"What size do you wear?"

"Thirty double A, but I want the kind with padding."

"Me too," I say.

"Certainly," the lady says, and starts hunting through the boxes behind the counter.

I have two bras at home. Hand-me-downs, of course,

from when Liz was my age. They're sort of crummy-looking, more like pieces of undershirts than real bras, and I hardly ever wear them. Besides, they're too big, not in the front but around the back. I know I don't really need them that bad. Still, a whole lot of the girls in my class have them and my mother said I could, too, but she wants me to start with Liz's old ones.

Maybe if I find a nice one here she'll let me buy it.

The lady gives us one apiece and says we can try them on.

There's only one dressing room, and it's not even a real room. All it is is a corner with a curtain hanging in front. And the curtain doesn't even cover the whole space because it's too short on the sides and everybody can see in.

Not exactly everybody, because the only person in the store is the lady who runs it, but anybody could walk in any time—even some of the boys in my class. Probably none of them would unless maybe they were picking up a package for their mothers or something. But I know I really don't want to take off my T-shirt because I'm not wearing an undershirt today and even if the lady doesn't look, still I don't want Jane to. Liz thinks it's hysterical that I'm so shy about anyone seeing me without my clothes on but she doesn't understand anything ever.

I wouldn't mind so much if I had something to hide, but I'm almost completely flat except for a tiny little bit of a bump around the nipples, especially the right one, which makes it even worse.

I think Jane is sorry she started the whole thing too, because we're stuck in this tiny space and there's no way we can have any privacy. I don't want it to look like I'm shy, so I do a lot of little things with the bra—like examining the stitches or trying out the elastic, and all the time I'm waiting for Jane to do something but all she does is the same thing as me—pretend she's interested in the bra. We might have to stand here forever. I know I'm definitely not taking my shirt off unless she takes hers off.

"If you want," she says, "I'll hold the curtain closed while you try yours on." And she turns around and holds the curtain and she doesn't even try to peek. I do practically the whole thing under my T-shirt anyway. Then I hold the curtain for her, and then we both put our T-shirts back on, and it looks terrific. A little pointy but fantastic and real, too.

"Are you going to buy it?" I ask Jane.

"I could," she says. "I have some birthday money my Aunt Hanna gave me. She'd die if I spent it on a bra, but I wouldn't have to tell her. What about you?"

I frown. "I can't. I just spent a whole load of money on my mother's birthday."

"I can lend you some. How much do you have?"

"Two dollars and twenty-five cents, but I may have another fifty-seven cents in my penny bank."

"It's only four fifty, so I could lend you the other two."

"But it's your birthday money."

"That's okay."

"I don't know. . . ." I try not to let her know how much I really want the bra so I just tell her maybe I'll save up and get it next month.

"Come on," she says, and her face brightens. "I don't

need the money for a long while, and besides, I would never have the nerve to be the only one wearing it. So if you don't buy it I'm not going to either. And I really want it."

She makes it sound like I would be doing *her* a favor so I say okay and she says great and we get dressed and I give her my two dollars and twenty-five cents and she pays for both bras.

"Let's go home to my house and put them on," Jane says, and before I can say yes she's dragging me down Eighth Street toward Sixth Avenue. I'm so excited about the bra that I've forgotten about the bike until I see a kid riding one down the street. Then I start to think about it and I get worried and scared all over again. I probably should go back to the park and look around some more, except now I have to go with Jane because she lent me the money, so I can't back out now.

"I have a whole load of sisters and only one brother," Jane says as we walk toward her house.

"I have one older brother and a sister and they're both awful," I tell her.

She says she's the baby, too, and that she has three sisters and that her brother, Charles, is a year older than horrible Neddy. We turn the corner onto West Ninth Street. It's one of the prettiest blocks in Greenwich Village, lined with lots of trees and beautiful old brownstone houses.

"Isn't it awful to be the littlest?" I ask Jane. "I hate the way everybody picks on me all the time."

"I don't think it's so bad," Jane says. "That's my house up there. The one with the geraniums." It's great-looking but I'm more interested in her brother and sisters. "But don't they all try to push you around?" I ask.

"Sure, they try to but I don't let them, except sometimes I get pushed around anyway. Everybody does sometimes."

"It's all the time for me."

"How come?"

"I guess it's because I'm little so I can't fight back."

"You mean they beat you up?" Jane looks really horrified.

"No, nothing like that," I answer as we climb up the front stoop. "They just tease me and then they pick on me all the time and . . ."

"But how come you don't fight back?"

"How can I? They're so much bigger than I am."

"What difference does it make how big they are if you don't have to punch them?"

"I don't know but it makes a difference. They're a lot older and smarter and I can't ever win over them."

"You know, Ari, I guess I don't feel that kind of little. I mean, the kind where you think you're always going to lose. In fact, most of the time I start off thinking that I'm going to win over them and a lot of the times I do." She pokes around in her jean pockets for her keys.

"Maybe my sister and brother are meaner than yours," I say.

"Are you kidding! Nobody could be more horrible than my brother Charles. Except lately he doesn't mess around with me so much and even Regina—she's only thirteen months older than me and I have to share a room with her—she hardly ever bugs me any more.

Mostly she bugs my oldest sister Beverly. Besides, I think the reason they pick on me and all that is because they're jealous of me."

"Why?"

"Because I'm the youngest," she says, and she really looks surprised that I didn't know. But I still don't know. Why would they be jealous because she's the littlest when that's the worst to be? So I ask her.

"First of all," she says, "it's special to be the youngest, and only one person can be it, and that one person is me."

She really sounds proud, as though she's saying she won a contest or something.

"And then there's all the things you get," she goes on. She finds her keys and opens the front door. We're in a small, neat vestibule.

"You mean the hand-me-downs?" I can hardly believe my ears.

"Right. Eventually I get everybody else's clothes plus all my own things. I've got the most anybody's ever had in my whole family. How about you?" she asks as she opens another door into a really great-looking hallway with deep red carpeting and a white staircase leading upstairs.

"Yeah, I guess I have too," I say. "I have Liz and Neddy's old things and my own stuff, so I guess I have the most of everyone too." Funny, I never thought about hand-me-downs like that.

"That's why they're all so jealous."

I'm going to have to think about that because I sure don't feel as terrific as Jane does about being a baby.

But she does make it sound pretty good.

Jane's family lives on the first two floors of the brownstone. When we go up the stairs and enter the apartment, her sister Regina, the one she shares the room with, is home and so is her sister Jackie, who looks about Liz's age. Jane introduces me and they both grunt out something that sounds like hello and that's all. They don't act any nicer than Liz would. I mean she would say hello to most of my friends, too, except the ones who have older brothers. Then she's all lovey-dovey. In fact, she makes it look like she likes them better than me, which isn't so great anyway.

Jane takes me into the kitchen, where her mother is making dough for an apple pie. She introduces us.

"Mommy, this is Ari. My new friend."

You see? She likes me. Not like with Rhona where I'm the one who does all the liking. This is much better.

I give her mother an especially big smile and put out my hand and say, "Hi. It's nice to meet you." That's what you're supposed to do when you meet someone for the first time but I never usually do except this time I want to make a very good impression.

"It's nice to meet you too, Ari." Mrs. Richardson shakes my hand. "Oops," she says, "sorry." And we all three laugh because now my hand is white with flour.

"Mommy, can I show Ari how I make dough in the Cuisinart?"

"Absolutely," Mrs. Richardson says, pointing to the sink, "but wash up first, Muffin."

What did I tell you? She really does look like a muffin.

Jane does a quick wash-up and then starts piling ingredients into the food processor. She turns and smiles at me. "Did you ever make dough in one of these things?"

"Nope," I say.

"Wait till you see. It's practically like magic."

She doesn't even look once at the recipe, and when she has everything in, she puts the top on, flips the switch, and steps back to watch. It *is* like magic. First it just spins around like it's not doing much, then the eggs and the flour and all start sticking together on one side, and then just when you think it's going to break down it makes a funny noise and the dough begins to form a ball that gets bigger and rounder with every whirl. Jane leaps for the switch and turns it off, opens the top and takes out a perfect ball of dough.

"Tra laa!"

I applaud. "That's fantastic."

Jane hands the dough to Mrs. Richardson, who wraps it in plastic and pops it into the refrigerator. "What have you girls been up to this morning?"

"We went shopping," Jane tells her.

"Oh?"

"For bras," I add.

For a second she doesn't say anything. Then she says, "Did you get any?"

We both nod, and then she asks if she can see what we bought.

"Come on, Ari." Jane pokes my arm. "Let's try them on for my mother."

"Okay." And I follow her out of the kitchen and into her bedroom.

Jane's room looks like mine except that the walls and the carpet and the curtains and bedspread and everything are all different shades of pale blue, not ugly red and yellow like mine. We both have posters, only mine is Kiss and hers is Rolling Stones, and a cork board for important notes, and she has bunk beds, too, even if mine is only for sleep-overs. But she shares the room with her sister so she really needs them. I can guess right away which bed is hers. The top bed is much nicer. It's all done up to look sort of Indian, so Jane's must be the bottom one, because, like I said, when you're the littlest kid you always get stuck with the worst choice.

"You sleep on the bottom, right?" I ask her, but I don't have to because I already know.

"Nope." She shakes her head. "I've got the top bunk."

"How'd you manage to do that?" I ask. I'm really surprised.

Jane smiles. "Regina grabbed the bottom one first."

"But the top one is so much better," I say. "How come she let you get it?"

"Mostly because it didn't look like that when we were choosing. It was just regular, but I did all those things, and now she's always bugging me to let her use it, so we finally made a deal, and she's going to get the top bunk at the end of this month."

"I would hate to give up that terrific bed."

"I don't care because I really want the bottom one, and besides, I have this fantastic idea of how to make the bottom bunk into a kind of tent. Is Regina going to be jealous when she sees that!"

"I'll bet she will," I say, and I really mean it because it's a great idea. I wouldn't ever think of doing something like that. Not that I can't. I'm pretty good at art and I even like to do projects. But I still wouldn't think of it because I'd probably be so disappointed and unhappy that I got the top bunk right in the beginning that I'd still be crying about it.

I can see that Jane is a lot like me in a lot of ways but there's something that's very different (good different, not bad) about her. It has to do with things like the beds and the way she feels about her family. She just doesn't seem as unhappy as I am. I don't know why. With all those sisters and another mean brother I know I would hate it here just like at home.

We change into our new bras (of course not in front of each other—she's just like me in *that* way) and then we stand around looking in the mirror so we can see what it looks like from every angle. I think it makes the T-shirt look terrific. We both love it.

"Let's go show my mother," Jane says, and we go downstairs to the kitchen. On the way through the dining room we have to pass Jackie and she screams, "I don't believe it! Regina! You've got to come see this."

It's just what Liz would do, be really mean, and then she would make fun of me and laugh and make me feel so bad that I'd start to cry. Then my mother would say something like "I told you not to tease Ari," and Liz would stop, except that she'd keep making faces behind my mother's back and I'd keep crying and finally I'd get in trouble.

But that's not what happens in Jane's house. That's

what I mean. Jane is different. She faces right up to her older sister. "You're practically sixteen, and you don't even have half as much," she says to Jackie, real snotty, and then she pokes me and says, "Ironing board," and *she* gets hysterical, and so do I.

The fantastic thing is that her sister gets very aggravated and ends up saying things like "You don't know how much I have, and you better keep your mouth shut in front of strangers or I'm telling Mama."

Then Jane sticks her chest out real far and we both strut right through the dining room, only now her sisters aren't laughing so hard and the older one wants to know how much we paid for it and can she try it on.

"Fat chance," Jane snaps, and we stalk off.

Jane's sisters are both a whole lot like Liz. You can tell they think they're hot stuff, especially Jackie because she's very pretty. She's got herself all dressed up like the forties with red lipstick and her hair pulled back to one side. She sort of looks like a model. Regina isn't so pretty and she's even skinnier than me. They both have the same dark brown hair and the same sour look on their faces. Liz gets that look when she tells me how I can't borrow anything or touch anything of hers.

As soon as we get out of that room, Jane says she can't stand the way her sisters bug her. But in front of them she never let on that they bothered her at all. I'm sure they didn't even know. Even *I* didn't know. I have to try to remember how she did that. Maybe I could try that kind of thing on Liz.

Mrs. Richardson has finished rolling the dough and is piling the apples in the pie shell. From the expression on her face she doesn't seem as if she's so crazy about the way we look in our new bras.

"Girls," she says, and you can tell something not so good is coming, "I don't know how to tell you this . . ."

Oh, boy, and I thought it looked so beautiful.

". . . but even though it fits well, it just doesn't look natural."

"You mean it looks stuffed?" Jane asks.

"Well, more like bought."

"Not grown, huh?" I ask.

"Definitely not grown. It would be very unusual for girls your age to be so well-developed, and then the shape is a bit too . . . too contrived."

"What do you mean, Mom?"

Right at that second this boy comes into the kitchen. He looks about fourteen, tall and skinny as a rail, and he's wearing a jogging suit and has a white sweat band around his head.

"She means you look like you're packing torpedoes," he says. And he makes firing noises that crack him up. He's just like Neddy. He has to be her brother, Charles.

"Mama," Jane says, "Charles is embarrassing Ari."

"Charles, please," Mrs. Richardson says, "we have a guest." She introduces us. He grunts something and then stares at my chest and rolls his eyes. I'm beginning to think the bra is a bad idea, and I wish I could get out of the kitchen. I look down at my chest, and the horrible things look gigantic, and when I look at Jane's they look even worse. I think they grew. Her chest is bigger than her mother's.

"Okay, Charles," Mrs. Richardson says, "zoo time is over. Take a glass of juice and beat it."

He gulps the juice, and all the time he's rolling his eyes and stifling a laugh, which I think is terrible. He's even worse than Neddy. I don't think Neddy would ever act that way in front of a guest. Not with my mother watching, anyway. I would be crying by now if he was my brother but all Jane does is stand there with her hands on her hips and just stare him down as if he were some kind of nutty freak. She doesn't say one word. After a little while I can tell he's beginning to feel sort of jerky, and finally he shrugs and goes out of the room. I think Jane won that battle and she didn't even seem to try. I would like to act like that when Neddy teases me. I'm going to remember the way she did it.

"I don't think the lady will let us return the bras, Mama," says Jane.

"Did you get them at that lingerie shop on Eighth near Sixth?" her mother asks.

"The one with the red-and-white awning," Jane says.

"That's the one. I bought panty hose there last week, and I saw a slip that I liked. Maybe I can return the bras and use the credit for the slip."

"What do you think, Ari?" Jane asks me.

"That would be great," I say.

"I hate mine too," says Jane.

"Okay then, girls. Don't worry. Take them off right now and make sure to fold them nicely when you put them back in the boxes. I'm sure I'll be able to get your money back. I'll run them over soon as I finish the pie. You girls hungry?"

"A little," says Jane. "How about you, Ari?"

I haven't been hungry since the bike was stolen. I guess it made me forget all about food. But now that I think of it I'm starving, so I say, "Yeah, I could eat," and her mother says if we want she'll make us peanut butter sandwiches.

We change out of the bras and wrap them up as nicely as we can. It's lucky we didn't take the tickets off yet. By the time we get back down to the kitchen the sandwiches are ready.

"Make sure you put your dishes in the sink, please, Jane," her mother says. "I'm going to take care of those things right now. Nice to meet you, Ari. Hope we see you again soon," and she takes the bra packages and leaves the kitchen.

The minute the front door slams Regina comes into the kitchen. I can tell she's going to start something. Just from the way she's smiling.

She says to Jane, "Mama make you take the bras back?"

"None of your business," Jane answers, but she doesn't look at her which seems to annoy Regina.

"Now who's an ironing board?" she teases.

"All three of us," Jane says, "but we're only eleven. How old are you?"

I can't get over the way Jane gives it right back to all of them. I would love to be able to do that but I just know I couldn't. They'd make me cry first.

"Make sure you don't leave one dish in the sink or I'll tell Mama," Regina says angrily. "I swear, you're such a little slob." She tosses her head back and stomps out of the room.

You see? Jane just won again by making her sister angry. She's really something. I can hardly believe she's only my age the way she's always winning over everybody.

After we finish the peanut butter I tell Jane that I have to get home because I didn't say I would be gone this long and my parents will be worried. They worry easily, I tell her.

"Are you going to be busy this afternoon?" she asks, and I tell her no and then she says maybe we could do something together. I love that idea so I ask her if she wants to come home with me just to check in and then we can do whatever she wants.

"Terrific," she says. "I'll leave my mother a note. But I'd better write down your telephone number just in case."

I always have to leave my number too, so her mother must be like mine that way. I told you a lot of things about Jane and me are the same, except, I don't know, she makes it look better. I wish I knew how she did it.

When we get back to my house, my parents still aren't back. Liz and Eddie are in the kitchen, drinking iced tea. Liz says Daddy called and said they were having lunch at the Sabatinos' and later they were going to play tennis with them so they wouldn't be back until about four. I'm happy about that because I dread the moment I have to lie about the bike. I never could lie real good to my parents. I know they'll be able to tell. I just know it.

I introduce Jane to Liz and Eddie. Eddie smiles and says hello and even stands up to shake Jane's hand. Liz grunts "hi" without even looking up from her nails.

She's polishing them, in between sips of her tea, probably for the fifth time today. One time I counted her nail polishes, and she had forty-six bottles. My father says that if she devoted half the time she spends on her nails to her school work she would be a brain surgeon already. Naturally, she never lends me one single bottle of polish ever.

Eddie is nice and friendly, but of course he's not my brother. My brother is a jerk. All Neddy says when I introduce him to Jane is that I should keep her out of his room, as if anybody in the world would ever want to go into that disgusting place unless the rest of the apartment was on fire or something.

Then he starts teasing me and pretending to shove a microphone into my face. "She's back, ladies and gentlemen, that brilliant bike sleuth, the great bucked-tooth wonder, Ari Jacobs."

"Come on, Neddy, leave me alone."

But he won't stop. Instead he goes right into his Nazi act. "Dumfkoph! Are you telling me zat you did not find zee bike?"

"Neddy, I swear I'm going to tell on you."

He puts his face right up to mine and gives me a stare like steel. "Vot haf you done vis zee bike!"

"Neddyyyy . . ."

"Vere is it!"

He's so mean. He never stops until he makes me cry. I know Jane's watching me, and I know if it was her she would make it all come out differently but I just can't. I can feel the tears starting to grow in my eyes and there's nothing I can do to stop him, and what's making me feel even worse is that I'm going to cry in front of my new friend.

"Didn't you say you had an older brother?" Jane suddenly asks me. "About fourteen years old or something?"

"That's him," I say, and I'm so surprised that she asked me that funny question that the tears jump back into my head.

"*He's* fourteen?" she says, like I'm crazy.

Now Neddy is suddenly interested, and he says, "What did you think?"

"Forget it," Jane says. But naturally he can't now.

"You figured I was about . . . sixteen, huh?" he says, and he's practically gloating. Something's funny. I don't know what, but I know Jane better now and I can tell she's up to something.

"Are you kidding!" She starts to giggle.

Oh, boy, I know what she's doing!

"What's so funny?" Neddy asks her.

Now Jane can hardly talk she's so hysterical. "Sixteen! You must be kidding! I thought you were twelve . . . I'm sorry, but you're so short I just thought . . ."

Neddy looks as though someone hit him in the face with a dead fish. "What are you talking about? I'm fourteen. I was fourteen two months ago. Tell your jerky friend, Ari. Tell her I'm fourteen."

Now I see how it works. I think.

"If he wants to say he's fourteen, it's okay with me," I say, looking straight at Jane.

"What do you mean it's okay with you! Are you nuts! You know I'm fourteen. Tell her!"

All I do is shrug. It's amazing, because that's really all I do, and he gets so angry that he screams the F word at me and storms out of the room.

I can't believe it. That was the first time in my whole life that I ever won over Neddy. I did, too. And I didn't even cry. Almost. Now I give Jane a great big smile and tell her thanks, and she says it's nothing, she does it all the time. I think she's the most terrific friend I ever had in the world. She's even better than Rhona because I think she even likes me too.

"Hey, Ari," Jane asks, "what's all that stuff about a bike?"

Before I get a chance to answer somebody rings the intercom buzzer from the lobby and Liz screams somebody better answer it. She never gets up to do anything. Someday she's going to forget how to walk. Neddy's still mad so he shouts to let Toad Face (that's me) answer it. So I pick up the intercom phone.

"Hello?"

"Mrs. Jacobs?" It's Frank, the doorman.

"No, this is Ari."

"Two policemen down here are coming up."

"Ohhh . . ." I know I sound like a squealing cat, but I'm so scared I can't find my normal voice.

I knew it.

They found out.

They're going to arrest me and take me away. I knew it would happen. My forehead is all sweaty, and my knees feel like they're made of rubber bands. I have to grab the wall just to keep standing.

"Should I send them up?"

"Yes." The only part that comes out is a little hiss at the end.

"What's that?"

"I said okay."

I turn around and lean against the wall. All of a sudden I have the worst headache I ever had in my life and I wish my mommy was here because I'm so scared.

"What's the matter, Ari?" Jane asks, and she puts her hands on my shoulders like she's helping me stand up. She asks me if I'm sick but all I can do is shake my head no. "Should I call your sister?" I shake my head quickly and stammer, "No, no, I'm okay."

"Who was it?" Jane asks. I can tell she's puzzled.

"The police. They're coming up about the stolen bike."

"Somebody stole your bike? Oh, that's too bad. I didn't know."

"It's not my bike. It's Liz's."

"It's not yours?" Jane sounds surprised. "I just thought from the way you looked—I mean, you look so upset."

"I am. Sort of. I guess. Mostly because this kind of thing never happened to us before. I mean, with the police and all." Then I tell her the whole story. Not the real one, the made-up one about the robbers taking the bike from the basement.

I hate having to tell my new best friend a lie but I have to because she would probably hate me if she knew what I did.

The police take forever to get upstairs. In the meantime I'm trying as hard as I can not to cry. By now

Neddy and Liz and Eddie are all waiting at the front door. Even Jane is up with them. I'm the only one hanging back in the hall, but I know it won't do any good because they're going to come right in and arrest me anyway. I hope they don't put handcuffs on me because then all the neighbors would see. Maybe they won't if I swear to them that I won't try to run away. But maybe they have to because it's the rules. If I put my poncho on, then that would hide the handcuffs except that everybody would probably wonder why I'm wearing a heavy poncho when it's so hot out. They'd probably think I was doing it to hide the handcuffs. I know that's what I would think if it was somebody else. I wish so hard it *was* somebody else. Anybody . . .

Liz doesn't even give the police a chance to ring the doorbell. As soon as she hears the elevator door she flings open our door.

It's the same two policemen as last time. Fitzroy, the one with the rosy cheeks, and the angry mean one, Jones, with the beer belly and the red face. I don't know why he looks so angry. It's not *his* bike.

The nicer cop, Fitzroy, asks, "Anybody else home?"

"No," says Liz.

I know they're looking for me, so the first thing I do is step back a little farther into the dark part of the hallway where they can't see me. What I really and truly want to do is hide in the kitchen cabinet under the sink. That's where I go when we play hide-and-seek, and they practically never find me. The game usually ends with me still under the sink so maybe if I hide there the policemen will think I went out and then they'll go home.

"Where's that other little kid?" the mean one asks, looking around.

If I'm going to get to the kitchen I have to run right now, but I can't. It's like I'm stuck to the floor. And now I'm crying.

"Ari, come here," Liz says, as though she's really annoyed. My own sister is going to turn me in. I didn't think she hated me *that* much. Now they're all looking at me and it's too late to do anything so I go right up to them with my hands out for the handcuffs. I don't want them to be madder at me than they are already.

"Cut the clowning, kid," Fitzroy says to me, then turns to Jane. "Who are you?"

"She's my friend," I say, hoping my voice doesn't croak like a frog.

He stares at her a moment, then asks Liz, "What about your folks? When are they coming home?"

"Not till after three," Liz says. "Did you find out anything about my bike?"

"Yeah, a couple of things."

"Great!" she says, all excited. "What happened to it! Where is it?"

"Not so fast. We got some more questions to ask you."

"You didn't find it yet?" Liz asks, and she looks so disappointed that even I feel sorry for her.

"Not yet, but we got some very interesting ideas about how your bike got stolen."

"Like what?" Neddy asks.

"Like maybe the thief didn't have to break the lock."

"But the chain was broken. . . ." Liz is beginning to sound puzzled.

"That was an old chain, and it was broken a long time ago," says Officer Jones. "My guess is that the thief put that piece of chain there just to throw us off his track." Now both cops are staring at Eddie.

I knew they would find out. And now they're trying to trick me into confessing by pretending they think Eddie knows. I'm going to confess anyway. I have to because I can't stand how awful this makes me feel. It's so terrible being a criminal. It's the worst thing in the world.

"Officer?" I squeeze past Neddy and pull on the nicer policeman's sleeve.

"Hold on, kid," he says without even looking at me. "Whoever took that bike knew the combination."

"That can't be," Liz says, "because nobody but us knows the combination."

"Right," Jones, the mean one, says, and he's still looking at Eddie, who's getting so uncomfortable that he's beginning to sweat. I can see his hair sticking to his forehead. Just like mine.

"How about your boyfriend over there? He knows the combination too. Doesn't he?"

"Of course," Liz says. And she's real angry because she's always sensitive when it comes to Eddie.

"Who else?"

"I don't know, my family, I guess."

"I don't know any combination," Jane says really fast. She looks a little nervous too. Policemen make you feel guilty even if you're not.

"That's right, she couldn't," Liz says.

"She around here much?" Jones wants to know.

"That's all we need," Neddy says, and Jane says to him, "What's that supposed to mean?" She's really something. She's not afraid of anyone.

I decide it's time to speak up. "This is the first time she's ever been to my house in her whole life," I say. You have to stand up for your friends. Even if you are a criminal.

"Okay, okay," Jones says. "We want to talk to Gonzalez here."

"What about?" Eddie doesn't like the looks of things. But I don't know why they're pretending to be so interested in Eddie when I know it's me they want.

"Tell me again where you were this morning."

"At band practice, I told you," Eddie says. "Then I went home, and then I came here. That's all. I didn't go anyplace else."

"Who were you with at band practice?"

"He was with me," Liz says, "and then he had to go home because his reed broke."

"What broke?"

"My reed," Eddie says. "I play the oboe and I went home because I thought I had an extra reed at home."

"What time did you leave practice?"

"I don't know." Eddie shrugs and looks at Liz. A few wet beads are on his forehead. And I'm beginning to feel terrible for him.

"It was right in the beginning of practice," Liz says. "A little after nine—I don't know, maybe ten after?"

"Yeah, about then," Eddie says. And he sounds a little angry. Or maybe scared.

"That's when you left?"

"I told you I went home to get a reed."

"At ten after nine."

"Right, at ten after nine. What's the matter with that?"

I'm so busy listening to all this that I forget that the policemen are supposed to be doing all this just to trick me. But now I think maybe I'm wrong. Maybe they don't want me at all because maybe they really think Eddie did it. That would be horrible if they thought Eddie stole the bike. Then I'd really have to tell. Except it doesn't look too bad yet. I mean, all they're doing is finding out where Eddie was and he's telling them so it'll probably be all right.

Then Officer Fitzroy, the nicer policeman, who isn't turning out to be all *that* nice, asks Eddie what time he got back to practice and Eddie says he didn't go back. Now Officer Jones jumps in.

"You telling us that you walked out at ten after nine and that's the last anybody sees you?"

"It's not like that," Eddie says. "I went home. My brother saw me there."

"What time did you get here?" Officer Fitzroy asks.

"I don't know," Eddie says, all confused.

"Don't you ever look at your watch?"

"Huh?"

"Forget it. Was it before twelve?"

"I guess so . . . maybe about eleven or eleven-thirty . . ."

"Eleven-thirty, I remember," Liz butts in. "What difference does it make? Eddie didn't steal the bike, so what difference does it make what time he got here?"

"That's close to two and a half hours," the mean cop says, not paying any attention to what Liz said. "What were you doing home all that time?"

"Nothing . . . goofing around. I don't know. . . ."

"Who else was home besides your brother?"

"I don't know . . . nobody, I guess."

"Which is it—I don't know or nobody?"

Eddie looks around as though he wants to run away, but with those two big policemen he can't. Finally he hangs his head down like he was admitting to a terrible crime and says, "Nobody, just my brother."

I hate what they're doing to Eddie. And besides what's wrong with only his brother being home?

"I think maybe we better have a talk with that brother of yours," Officer Jones says, and he starts to sort of shove Eddie toward the door.

"Hey, wait!" Liz says, grabbing Eddie by the arm and pulling him back into the room.

"Yeah, wait!" Neddy joins in, putting himself in front of Eddie. "Where are you taking him?"

Oh, I wish my mommy and daddy were home. They wouldn't let this happen. I just know it. I have to do something. It's all my fault. I can't let them take Eddie away like that. He didn't do anything and the only reason they're blaming him is that he's Puerto Rican. I know a lot of people connect crime to Puerto Ricans in New York City—people like that mean policeman. Right from the beginning he didn't like Eddie and he even made fun of him a little because you could tell he wasn't part of our family. I hate that awful policeman.

"Okay, kid," the cop says, "let's get moving."

"Wait! Wait a minute!" That's me, and I'm running out from behind everyone, and I go right up to the mean policeman. I just can't stand what they're doing to Eddie any more. "It's not his fault, he didn't do it," I shout.

Everyone turns and stares at me.

"I did it," I gasp, and I really and truly think I'm going to pass out.

NINE

"Calm down, will you, kid?" Officer Fitzroy says. "What do you mean it's your fault? What did you do?"

"I did it! I got the bike stolen. . . ." Now they're all looking at me. Liz hardest of all.

"How?" Liz says. "What are you talking about, Ari?"

Everybody's trying to ask me questions at the same time and nobody's giving me a chance to talk. And I'm not sure I know what I want to say. Maybe I shouldn't have started this. But I had to.

I had to because I couldn't watch them doing that to Eddie.

"Okay, okay, quiet down, everybody, and let the kid talk," Officer Fitzroy says, practically shouting. Everybody gets very quiet and now they're all waiting for me to say something. I take a big breath and repeat real loud and clear as I can:

"I did it."

"What did you do?" Liz is practically screaming in my face. "For God's sake, tell me. What did you do with my bike!"

"I forgot to lock it."

"You forgot to lock it? What are you talking about?"

"The last time I used it. I didn't close the locks. I'm sorry, I really am."

Liz gets a blank look on her face. "You never . . ." But she stops right in the middle of her own sentence. She was probably going to say something about how I never used her bike in my whole life. But she doesn't. She just looks hard at me for a minute and then says, perfectly naturally, "You should be more careful next time."

If the police knew Liz at all they would know something was fishy, because if she really thought I left the locks undone she'd kill me right there and then, even with them watching. Probably scream me to death or something.

"Let's get this clear, kid," Officer Fitzroy says. "When did you use the bike last?"

"Yesterday in the afternoon I took it . . . uh . . . for a ride."

"Where?" the mean cop says so fast he makes me gulp.

"Around . . ."

"Around where?"

". . . the corner."

"That's right." Neddy jumps in. "She took it for a ride yesterday afternoon. I remember."

"How long were you gone?" Jones asks. He sounds as though he doesn't quite believe me.

Neddy and I answer his question right at the same second, only I say an hour and he says a half hour.

But Liz saves us. "That's right," she says, real fast. "She had my bike for an hour and a half."

"And when I came back," I say quickly, "I put it in the storage room and then later when it got stolen I remembered that I didn't lock it, but I was afraid to say anything." I turn to my sister with a sheepish look. "I'm sorry, Liz," I say to her, and I really mean it, except not the way she thinks.

"That's all right, honey," she says, and her mouth isn't laughing, but her eyes are practically hysterical.

I don't know how come the policemen don't know that something funny is going on but they don't because the nicer one just shrugs and says that's what happens when you leave an expensive bike unlocked. "Nothing we can do now," he says, "but keep our eyes open for it in case somebody tries to sell it."

But the mean one is really angry now. "You made us waste a lot of time. You could get into big trouble holding back information like that. You just remember that, kid, big trouble."

And he shakes his finger right in my face. It's a gigantic finger and I back up a little because if that ever hit my nose it would really hurt. I don't think policemen should do things like that. Most of them are nice. We have lots of really pleasant ones in my neighborhood.

But this one is mean, especially now that he can't get to take Eddie away. I think he really wanted Eddie to be the stealer and now he's angry because I ruined everything for him. I hope when it comes time to arrest me they send someone else. Just the thought of him coming for me makes my stomach turn.

I feel better, though, when I look at Eddie. I'm not saying he looks great, but at least he's not so scared and sweaty. Before, his face was all shiny and almost yellow, and it looked as if he was going to faint. But now he looks pretty okay.

The policemen tell us we should let them know if we hear anything or remember anything else, and the mean one looks right at me when he says that. In the meantime they tell us not to call them to inquire, they'll get in touch with us if there's any news.

We all thank them and sort of work them out of the house. The minute the door closes behind them Liz puts her finger to her mouth for us to be quiet. We wait until we hear the elevator doors close and then Liz lets out a big whoop! And everybody else says, "Wow! Yea!" and we all start jumping up and down and Liz grabs me and hugs me and kisses me all over my head and so do Eddie and Jane and Neddy.

They're all pounding me on my back and everybody's screaming how I'm fantastic! Terrific! Sensational! It's the best thing that ever happened to me. It's like I'm a hero. Liz says I am and Eddie says I saved his life practically and he'll never forget it and even Neddy says he can't believe that I'm smart enough to do what I did and how nobody else thought of it. And they're all going on and on and I feel so happy and proud that Jane is there to see this whole thing. I can tell she's really impressed.

"That was the nicest and smartest thing anybody could ever do," Liz says, hugging me again, "and I'm going to remember it always, Ari, and from now on you can borrow anything of mine or use my room or anything. That was incredible, what you did. Even I got fooled for a minute but then I remembered that I was definitely the last one to use the bike and I absolutely remember locking it and covering it and everything. That was brilliant, Ari, super-stupendous!"

And she smears another huge kiss right on my forehead!

Liz has never in my whole life as long as I can remember ever hugged me that much. She kissed me a few times when I was going away someplace when Mommy made her, and again one time when I fell off the top of her dresser and cut my leg bad. She kissed me and patted my head and all, but mostly I think she was worried I'd tell my parents because it was all her fault anyway. She had wanted me to get on the dresser so I could hold the top of her John Travolta poster. But this time she's doing it because she really loves me. I can tell. Right in the middle of feeling so terrific I start to think about what everybody would think if they knew the real truth. Ugh!

But I don't have to tell. Not yet, at least. So I'm not going to.

Later on, when I show Jane my bedroom, all she wants to do is talk about what a fantastic thing I did saving Eddie. It's beginning to make me very uncomfortable, all that talk about how wonderful I am. Especially hearing Jane say it so much because I really like Jane and I feel bad, as though I'm cheating her. It's just plain awful to lie. I hate the feeling it gives me, all squiggly and squirmy inside and bad all over. I wish I could tell Jane the truth and then maybe she could help me. I know it wouldn't be so bad if I could just tell somebody like Jane.

"Boy, Ari, I just know I would never have thought of taking the blame like that. They were dying to take Eddie away, especially the fat mean cop."

There she goes again. I can't stand it that she thinks I'm so great when I'm really horrible. She'd hate me if she knew the truth.

"Probably Neddy or Liz were going to do the same thing," I say, "only I beat them to it."

"Oh, no, you're wrong," she replies quickly. "You could tell nobody else thought of it. You were the only one, and it was so brave of you. I'd have been scared to death to do that with those awful policemen."

I keep telling her anybody would have done the same thing, but she keeps telling me how terrific I am. The more she says it the worse I feel.

I have to tell her the truth. No matter what.

"Jane," I say, "it's not like you think."

"I saw it. You practically saved his life."

"I didn't."

"You did."

"Not really, I mean, not like it looked."

"Ari, I think you're just being modest but you don't

have to be with me. Besides, you should feel proud about what you did. I would if I were you. In fact, I'm proud to be your friend."

Oh, God. I feel so awful. I can't stand it any more. I take a deep breath and blurt it out.

"I lied."

There. I said it.

"How?" Jane asks me.

"About the bike. Taking it and all."

"I know you did. That's what makes it so terrific. I mean that you thought it up so fast."

"You don't understand. I'm not talking about that lie. I mean the big one. About how the bike got stolen in the first place."

"Oh." That's all she says. Just "Oh." And then she becomes quiet and sort of waits for me to go on.

I dread telling her, because I know she's not going to like me any more. But I need to tell her the truth, so I do.

Right from the beginning.

And even though I know she won't want to be my friend ever again, it still feels better just to tell some-body. I guess I'm crying again but it's the first time I've been able to tell anyone the whole story.

"Oh, boy," she finally says, "that's horrendous."

"Yeah, I know." I could die.

"What are we going to do?"

"We?"

"Right. Now that you told me, I'm in it with you, and since you're my friend I have to help you."

"I thought you would hate me."

"I'd never hate you. Especially since you trusted me so much. Besides, maybe if there are two of us we can find the bike. When I lose something my father always says to me that I have to reconstruct the whole thing. What you do is start from the very beginning and try to remember everything that happened. And if anybody was there you have to remember that too."

We go over the story again. I tell her about the old man and the two boys who were tossing his hat and all that, and then she wants to know if anybody else saw what happened. I tell her about Bag Mary and Wendy. I don't know if they were watching, but they probably were because they don't have much else to do.

"Come on," she says, "let's go see if we can find Bag Mary."

TEN

We go back to the little park, and it's more crowded now. Mostly they're regular ordinary people, but some of the street people are there too, so we start to ask if anybody has seen Bag Mary and Wendy. But most of them don't even answer us. The first one we talk to is the Lysol Lady. She's an old lady who wears one of those surgical masks on her face and carries a can of Lysol all the time, and then before she sits on a bench or touches anything she sprays it with Lysol. She tells us a whole long thing about how many germs are in Wendy's head and mouth and how we're lucky if we don't find them because we'd probably catch beriberi, whatever that is.

Jane says thank you nicely to her, and we keep looking. We don't even ask the drummer, because he's so weird. All he does is hit the sidewalk with drumsticks all day long.

Everybody calls them crazies but I kind of like them. They do strange things but they can't help it and they never ever harm a soul.

It looks like they're all out today. Even Roller Rene is here and you hardly ever see her in the daytime. She's always dressed in olden-day clothes except that she wears white shoe roller skates and even when it's really hot out she's got her hands tucked into a raccoon muff. But the weirdest thing about her is that she's really a man. I didn't know until my father told me, because she looks just like a woman.

I ask her if she's seen Bag Mary and she smiles and does two beautiful figure eights and when she glides past me she leans down and whispers, "Not today." Then she's gone before I can ask her anything else. These street people are very strange but if they were regular I guess they wouldn't be skating around or playing the drums on the sidewalk.

We walk all through the park and ask a lot of people and then we even look down some of the streets around the park. We keep at it for almost two hours but we can't find Bag Mary.

"I'm sorry, Ari," Jane says, "but I can't do any more today because I have to be home by four. I have to help my mother with the party." Then she tells me that it's her birthday Monday, and even though it's just going to be a small party, with just her family, she'd really like me to stop by.

"It's no big deal," she says. "We're just going to have a buffet and some ice cream and cake and that kind of stuff. Everyone's going to be there around two. We only have a half day of school Monday, so you could come home with me. Please come. I really want you to."

"I have to ask my mother," I tell her, "but I'm sure she'll say okay. I'll call you later when I get home."

Then Jane says how she's so glad we got to be friends today and I say I'm glad too, and we make all kinds of plans for sleep-overs and movies and everything for the next month. Then she goes home and I'm so happy that I found the best friend I ever had in my whole life. If only I could talk to Bag Mary, then maybe I could find the bike and then everything would really be great.

I go sit in the part of the park where all the street people usually hang out. For a long time it's really quiet, with only one or two people around. Then about four-thirty some more people come, and I see Bag Mary and her dog Wendy coming in way down at the other end of the park. I get up and run as fast as I can to them. I'm all out of breath when I reach them, and I can hardly get my question out.

"Wendy," I say between huffs and puffs, "remember the morning those two boys were teasing that old man? You remember they were grabbing his hat and I tried to help him?"

"You sure did, honey," Wendy says. But of course it's really Mary. "That Bucky and his friend sure are nasty boys, making that old man cry like that. That was very nice, the way you helped him."

"Thank you, but I think while I was helping the old

man somebody took my bike, and it's not even mine, it's my sister's, and it's terrible because she called the police and all and I just have to get that bike back. Did you see the boys who took it?"

"Those are bad boys. I've seen them before but you better not get mixed up with them. It's too dangerous. Let the police take care of them."

"I will but first I have to talk to them. I really have to. . . . Please, could you tell me where they are?"

"I don't think you should go alone."

"Please . . . I have to know."

"Well, all I know is that one's called Bucky and I don't know where they are today. Sometimes I see them hanging around Delmonte's, the luncheonette over on Eighth Street near the shoe store."

"Oh, thank you, Wendy, I know which one."

"You better be careful, honey—those are very mean boys."

"I will, Wendy, I promise."

"One time they tried to steal the drumsticks from the old drummer, and they would have, too, except some neighborhood people saw what was happening and called the police so they ran away. But they're no good. That's all they are, so you better stay far away from them."

"I will. But first I have to find out what they know." I tell Wendy thank you and I even say thanks to Mary but she pretends she doesn't even know me so I just say good-bye again to Wendy. If only Bag Mary didn't do that thing with Wendy I guess she'd really be just like anybody else. I like her a whole lot. But she sure is peculiar.

I know where that luncheonette is because we used to go there all the time with my parents to get egg creams. That's that soda with chocolate syrup and milk and plain seltzer. I don't understand why they call it an egg cream when it doesn't have eggs or cream in it. My father said that he remembers it from when he was a little boy and it didn't have eggs or cream in it then either. And they say Bag Mary's nuts.

I go right to Delmonte's and there's nobody there except the old lady who runs the place. I have enough money for an egg cream, so I sit down at the counter and ask her for one. I feel like I'm in some kind of old movie—you know, where somebody gets all the information he needs when the people are doing simple things like making egg creams. So while she's mixing the soda for me, I ask her if she knows a boy named Bucky. She doesn't answer me or look up or anything so I ask her again and this time I say it really loud. But she still doesn't even look up from the soda.

I feel dumb asking her again so I just say, "Thank you anyway," and wait for her to finish making an egg cream.

"There you go," she says. "Now see if that's sweet enough for you."

I tell her it's just right, and she says, "Good," and smiles at me and she seems so nice I don't know why she wouldn't answer me when I asked her about Bucky.

I finish my egg cream and put the glass down on the counter. She sees me do it and comes over. "Want anything else, dear?" she asks.

"Could I have a glass of water please?"

"Sure thing," she says, and grabs a glass and starts

filling it. It's weird how nice she is when she talks to me and how mean she is about my questions. Except she did give me a glass of water, and she didn't seem to mind at all. Maybe if I tried to think like a real detective I could figure it out. Except that a real detective could order some more sodas and sit around all day and try to get to be her friend and all, and he could take all the time he wanted because his mother wouldn't be angry if he was home late for dinner.

A man about my father's age comes into the store. He picks up a *New York* magazine and comes over to the counter.

"How's it going, Annie?" he says, pushing the money over to her, but she ignores him. The man turns, and I expect him to be angry but all he does is smile at me and reach over and tap Annie on the shoulder. She looks up and gives him a great big hello and then he asks her again how it's going and this time she says not so good.

"Trouble with Bucky again?" he asks, and I almost fall off the stool because that's just who I'm looking for.

"There's no way to keep that boy in school," Annie says, shaking her head and making the *tsk tsk* sound adults make when things are really hopeless. "But he has to stay there until he's sixteen, and that won't be for another four months. Meanwhile that truant officer is around here every week like clockwork. I tell you I'm at my wits' end. What am I going to do with that boy?"

Now I feel like a real detective, the way I'm picking up all this information. Annie must be Bucky's mother. But how come she looks old enough to be his grandmother?

"How's your other grandson?" the man asks. Aha!

"Arnold is such a wonderful boy." Annie starts to smile as soon as she begins talking about Arnold. Anyone can see he's her favorite, the way she goes on about how he's a straight-A student and how he helps out in the store and works after school and he's so handsome and just everything. If I were Bucky I would probably hate Arnold or at least I'd be really jealous of him. It's funny to see how she makes such a bad face when she talks about Bucky and puts on such a happy smile for Arnold. It makes me sort of feel bad for Bucky because if your own grandmother doesn't like you then probably nobody else could even stand you. Well, maybe she's right, the way Bucky was so mean to that old man. Besides, I'm sure he stole the bike. And I still have to find out.

"Excuse me," I say to Annie, but she pays no attention. Only the man looks at me. I bet if I was Arnold she'd pay attention. I really know how Bucky must feel. "Excuse me, please," I say again, real loud this time.

"Annie," the man says after touching her arm. "I think the young lady wants to say something to you."

Now Annie turns to me and asks very nicely if she can help me. I am definitely going to be a detective because I think I'm very good at it. I just figured out how come Annie doesn't answer me except when she's looking right at me. I bet she doesn't hear so good and she only knows what you're saying when she's watching you talk. She lip-reads. Or reads lips. I'm not sure how you say it. But lots of deaf people can do it so good you hardly know that they're deaf. I couldn't tell about Annie till right this minute. Now I say to her, very slowly and clearly, making my whole face move with my mouth, that I'm a friend of Arnold's. She looks a bit surprised because I'm so little. But then she smiles, because if I'm a friend of Arnold's I must be okay. I guess you could say that was pretty tricky but I have to find Bucky, and besides, it's the kind of thing a real detective would do.

"Arnold said for me to tell Bucky to call him right away. He has something very important to tell him so could you tell me where Bucky is, please?"

"I wish I could, dear, but I never know where that boy is. The only thing I know for sure is that he's never where he's supposed to be."

"Is he coming back here today?"

"He better if he knows what's good for him."

"Do you think it'll be soon?"

She shrugs as though she has no idea in the world. "Maybe you could try the bowling alley. Sometimes he goes there. Or the little park. Or God knows where that boy goes." Then she turns to the man and says, "See what I mean, Mr. Gibson? Even his own brother can't find him."

"The bowling alley on Eighth Street?" I ask her after touching her arm.

"That's the one," she says. "But I can't say for sure he's there. You never know about that kid."

I slide off the stool, thank them very much, and head for the door. Just when I get to it Annie asks me where Arnold was this afternoon. But I pretend I don't hear her and get out into the street as fast as I can.

I've never been to a bowling alley alone in my whole

life. I don't think my parents would let me, and I feel bad doing it. But I have to find Bucky and all I'm going to do is just peek in and if I see him I can go right up and ask him about the bike. It's not as though I'm going to stay there for the whole afternoon, so it's really not so bad.

"Rollright Bowling Alley" is just halfway up the block from Delmonte's, upstairs in one of those crummy old buildings. The stairs are so old they're all caved in in the middle, and the walls in the halls are dirty with big globs of plaster falling off. Each step is so high I have to hold onto the railing just so I can get my leg up. I never saw such big steps. It must be a very old building or the people must have been really tall in the olden days or something.

The bowling alley is on the second floor and you can hear the roar of the balls and the smash of the pins from the hallway. It sounds like it's very crowded. There's a glass door, but the glass is so dirty you can't see through it. I have to wait outside the door for a while because maybe if someone comes out I can take a look in and then I won't have to go all the way in.

Nobody comes out for a whole five minutes. I know I'll never find Bucky if I stand out here, but I'm afraid that they'll throw me out if I go in because I'm too young. But finally I just push the door open because I feel so awful about the bike. So what if they yell at me or throw me out? It can't be any worse than being arrested for stealing your sister's bike.

It's a gigantic place and when I look around a whole load of boys look just like Bucky and his friend so I have to go all the way in and practically up to the alleys to see if they're there. I was sure it would be so easy to recognize those two awful boys. But now everybody's beginning to look alike.

"Looking for somebody, kid?" a man with some drinks on a tray asks me.

"I'm looking for Bucky," I say. "His brother Arnold wants him." It sounds real to me.

"Don't know any Bucky," he says, so it must sound real to him too. "What's he look like?"

"I don't know. Regular, I guess . . . brown hair and all that. About your height, I think. He's fifteen or so."

"That's some description, kid. There must be twenty guys in here look like your Bucky. Why don't you ask over at the shoe rental counter? It's way over on the other side near the lockers."

"Thank you," I say and head where he's pointing.

There's a girl at the counter but she says she doesn't know any Bucky. Then this other boy who's returning shoes asks me if I mean Bucky Lynch. I say I don't know his last name. He describes him and it sounds sort of like Bucky so I say, "Yeah, that's the one."

"He hangs out a lot at Reinhardt's bike shop over on East Fourth," he says, and my heart practically jumps out of my stomach. A bike shop! That's got to be it! I mean, where the bike is and Bucky and everybody. I don't know how, but it sounds like what I'm looking for. I get so excited because I'm sure I've practically found the bike and now everything's going to be all right. I say thank you to both of them and start running as fast as I can out of the bowling alley, down those steps so fast I couldn't stop if I wanted to.

It's about ten minutes down to the East Village and if my mother knew I was going there she would kill me. It's a weird place with a lot of dopers and Hell's Angels, you know, the real tough people who ride around on motorcycles and have chains and tattoos on them and they're ugly and dirty. I never saw a real one but I saw a movie on TV where this motorcycle gang takes over a town and everybody's real scared of them. If I see one of them I'll just die, I'll be so scared.

I reach East Fourth Street, but I don't see any bike store and I have to ask somebody. It's hard to figure out who to ask because I don't want to ask a Hell's Angel person and I don't remember exactly how they looked because that movie was a long time ago. And now almost everybody is beginning to look like I think I remember them looking so I just stand there waiting for a real kind of person to come along. Finally an old lady comes by but she doesn't speak English too well. Probably a lot of the people I see are really all right but by the time I make up my mind to ask them they're already gone so I just stand there like I'm dumb or something. I've got to do it now! No matter what, I'm going to ask the next person who passes.

"Excuse me, mister," I say to a man in a leather jacket with a straggly awful beard, "could you please tell me where Reinhardt's bike store is?"

"Ya see dat corner over dere?" I can hardly hear him because even though he doesn't have his chains with him I know he's a Hell's Angel person and I'm really scared a whole lot.

He's saying something about the corner to me so I nod and pretend like I'm looking over at it. "Ya go down dere two stores and dere it is. Ya see, kid?"

"Yes, sir," I say, gulping all the time.

"Want me ta take ya?"

Now my heart slides right down to my knees and I shake my head like crazy.

"Whatever ya say, kid." And I can tell I insulted him and more than anything in the world I don't want to make him angry so I make my mouth squeeze open into the biggest, widest smile that ever was. It feels like my lips are going to touch my ears.

He looks at me as though I'm crazy, shrugs, and walks off.

The back of his jacket says, "Little League."

I didn't know the Hell's Angels had a little league.

I wait until he's out of sight, then I walk down to the corner and go down the block two stores and there's Reinhardt's. Besides everything else, I feel pretty good that I found this place all by myself, and it's the first time I've ever been down here in my life.

There must be a hundred bikes in the store and lots of them chained up outside and I just know Liz's bike is here and I feel so good I can't stop smiling. Maybe I won't even have to find Bucky, which would be very nice because he's such a terrible boy.

But what if the owner doesn't believe my story? I mean, suppose I go up to him and tell him he's holding my sister's bike by mistake and he just laughs in my face. He might too, you know, because like the police-man said maybe Bucky sold it to him for a lot of money. He might even tell me to go home, get lost, or something like that. If that happens, I guess I'm going to have to get very tough with him and tell him that if he doesn't give me back the bike I'm going to tell my father on him. That would probably scare him plenty, but just in case it didn't I'll tell him that I'm going to go right to the police.

Except if I did that I'd probably end up with those two awful cops from before and they'd start asking me a whole load of questions and then it would all come out, how I was the stealer and everything. Probably they'd put me on parole and then I'd have to report to a judge or somebody like that or even worse—oh, gross!—to **Liz**. Still, if my sister's bike is in there I have to know for sure so I cross my fingers, take a deep breath, and shove the door open.

I look around. There's only one man in the place and it must be Mr. Reinhardt, the owner. All of a sudden I think I must have made a mistake. He looks like such a nice, kind old man, just like a grandpa. He's got the pinkest skin and silky shiny white hair and his face is round and soft-looking like that little puffin pastryman on the TV commercial.

I go right up to him and say, "Excuse me, sir, could you help me please?"

"Get those grubby little hands off my bikes!" he snaps, swiping my hand off the bike. I wasn't even leaning on it hard. I was just touching it a little.

"What do you want?" he says in the same gross voice.

"Uh . . ."

"Well? Come on, speak up. I haven't got all day."

". . . uh, you see . . ."

"No, I don't see."

I can't believe it. This kindly old man is the meanest person I've met in my whole life and he's making me so nervous I can hardly get the words out of my mouth. "My sister's bike . . ." That's all that comes out before I'm crying and then I can't say anything.

Now he looks down at me real close as though he's suddenly interested in what I'm saying except that I'm not saying anything because of the crying. "What about your sister's bike?"

"Wha shea las ahme . . ."

"Stop bawling, will ya? I can't understand a word you're saying."

"It got lost . . . ahhh . . . in the park. Somebody took it."

Now he looks so angry I back away from him but I can't get too far because I bump into the bike behind me.

"Look, kid, I don't know anything about your sister's bike. I only sell new bikes. You wanna buy a new bike?"

I can't even get out a no, so I just shake my head and the tears jump off my cheeks and one of them lands on his shirt.

"Then beat it. . . ."

I don't wait for him to say anything else. I turn and go as fast as I can, even though I can hardly see where I'm running because of the tears.

He's saying something else but I can't make it out

because I'm running so hard. When I get to the corner I can still hear him yelling at me.

I run and cry all the way back to Eighth Street. I feel better when I get to Eighth Street, but it's later than I thought, so I keep running all the way back to my house. By the time I get there I'm not crying any more but I feel so unhappy because now I don't think I'll ever get that bike back.

It's dark when I get home, and my parents are in front of our building, waiting for me. Now I'm in even more trouble.

"Where have you been all this time!" my mother says, and she's got her hands on her hips and she's steaming mad. "How dare you stay out to this hour without even telling us where you're going!"

"I'm sorry . . . I'm sorry . . ." I start to say, but my father grabs me by the arm and pulls me into the lobby. They're both whisper-screaming at me while we wait for the elevator and all the time I'm crying and they don't even give me a chance to say where I was or anything.

All the way up in the elevator they say how they were just going to call the police and how could I be so inconsiderate and I'm going to be severely punished. Boy, they hardly ever both get so angry but I guess they were really nervous. That's what my father says. How could I pick such a terrible day to frighten them like that, what with the bicycle theft and all?

I tell them I'm sorry and that I went to my new friend's house and got lost coming home.

"Well, why didn't you call us?" my mother asks.

"I didn't have any money. . . ." I'm crying again.

Then my father says, "Don't you know you can always call the operator even if you don't have a dime?"

"I didn't know." I really didn't.

"Why doesn't she know that, Marilyn?" he asks my mother.

"I have no idea. I thought everyone knew that," my mother says.

"Well, she should have known," he says.

"Are you saying it's my fault that she didn't know?" Now my mother is getting annoyed at him and I'm thinking maybe they'll start arguing with each other and forget about me. But it doesn't work like that. They remember me and I get a long lecture about staying out late and making sure that I leave phone numbers when I go to a friend's house and all that, and then they ground me for next weekend. I don't say anything about Jane's party Monday afternoon because right now they would absolutely say no.

All anybody talks about at dinner is the bike. I don't say anything much. But Liz and Neddy tell the story of how I saved Eddie from the police. I should be happy because when they tell it I sound like a heroine from a book. Still all it does is make me feel sick around the stomach when anybody says anything about the bike. They all think it's so terrific what I did that they want to talk about it over and over again. I can hardly eat anything and it's my favorite—fried chicken. Even my parents are saying how proud they are of me. How courageous I was and all that. It's awful. I hate lying. It ruins everything.

"What's the matter, darling?" my father asks me. "Don't you feel well?"

"My head hurts a lot," I say, and then they get all concerned and my mother takes me into my room and helps me get into my pj's and into bed and she kisses me and hugs me. Then my father comes in and he does the same thing and then Liz does and even Ned comes in to say good night. I feel horrible. I liked it better when everybody used to pick on me. And besides, my head really hurts now from feeling so bad.

Everybody goes out and my father turns off the light and I put my head deep into my pillow so nobody will hear me crying.

Today was the worst day of my whole life.

ELEVEN

Sunday is a blur. We go to my grandparents' country club and all I do is mope around. I don't even get into my bathing suit and I don't even go into the steam room and I'm not even the littlest bit hungry all day long. We leave right after dinner because my parents say that maybe I'm coming down with something.

As soon as we get home my mother takes my temperature. She's surprised because it's normal.

"Ari dear, is something bothering you?" she asks me when I get into bed at eight-thirty without anyone telling me to.

"No, Mommy," I tell her, "I'm just tired."

She kisses me good night and tells me that she'll be in the living room reading if I want to talk to her.

As soon as she goes out, I turn off the light. I try to sleep but my mind keeps making up the same scene over and over again. It's one where Rhona tells me I have to borrow Liz's bike and I say, "Absolutely no!"

If only I really had said no to Rhona. If only . . .

TWELVE

I wake up three times in the middle of the night because of awful dreams. I only remember the last one because it was so real I thought it actually happened. I was in the park with the bike, only it was much smaller than Liz's bike and it kept getting littler and littler. Bucky was there and we were all watching it shrink. Even my grandparents. Then when it got as small as a nut I flipped it up and it fell right into my mouth. "Don't swallow it!" everybody shouted but it was too late. They all got so angry at me. Even Bucky, and it wasn't even his bike. I woke up all sweaty.

Breakfast is terrible. Liz keeps hugging me and Neddy doesn't even tease me once and my mother says all I have to have is a glass of milk if I don't want any breakfast. But my father makes me his special egg sandwich on a roll, which I always love, but today I can barely get it down. In fact, I hide half of it in my napkin.

When I tell them about Jane's party they say certainly I can go and my mother will pick up a present this morning and drop it off at school for me.

The only thing I really want is for the bike to be back down in the cellar. But when I check on my way to school, the spot is still empty. I never saw such an empty spot.

As soon as I get to school I remember that Rhona was really angry at me from the bike race business Saturday. I don't know which is worse, being home where everybody keeps hugging and kissing me or being here where Rhona is probably going to punch my head in or something even more horrendous than that.

I hope I see Jane before I run into Rhona. I told you how bad it is when Rhona's mad. But maybe if Jane is with me she won't push me around so much. I guess it's all according to who Rhona is today. If she's Florence Nightingale, I'm okay. With my luck it'll probably be Attila the Hun.

"Hey, dummy!" Oh, gee, it's Rhona. We're in the hallway outside the art room. "Do you know what you did to me Saturday?" she says with her hands on her hips and her face all squeezed up to look disgusted. The hallway is jammed with kids going to their classes.

"I'm really sorry, uh . . . Rhona?"

"Yeah," she says. "Who'd you think it was?"

I was hoping for Attila.

"I had to use Rachel's crummy old bike. I just barely qualified for the race because of you."

"Honest, I'm sorry." It seems I'm always apologizing to Rhona.

"I'll bet you are. You just don't care about anybody but yourself or you would have made it your business to get your sister's bike. Boy," she says, looking at her two sidekicks, Tracy and Margot, "is she selfish!"

"That's not true. I told you somebody took the bike. I brought it to the park. I really did."

"You think we're dumb enough to believe that anybody's going to steal a bike when you're standing right there looking at it?"

"I really hate liars," Margot butts in. And now a whole crowd of kids have stopped and are watching and I'm so embarrassed because I just know I'm going to cry.

"Me too," Tracy says, and then all three start saying how they can't ever believe anything I say.

"I swear I did," I say, and I know I sound like I'm begging but I don't want everyone to think I'm lying.

"Liar," Rhona says and I can feel the tears starting.

"I am not."

"Are too."

"She is *not* a liar," Jane snaps. I didn't see her coming down the hall, but here she is, stepping right into the middle of it all. And she talks right at Rhona.

"How do you know so much, smarty?" Rhona shoots right back at Jane.

"Because I saw it happen. That's how I know."

"Yeah," Rhona says, really tough because nobody

ever messes with her. "Well, maybe you don't see so good."

"Yeah, well, maybe you don't ride a bike so good." Now Jane sounds tough too.

"Says who?" Rhona practically spits it out right in Jane's face. Everybody moves in closer. There must be dozens of kids watching. Nobody's ever been this brave with Rhona before. Not even the boys. And Jane is practically exactly my height so it's really scary.

"Says me, that's who." Everybody in the hall is silent, expecting a fight. "And by the way, I think everyone should know that except for two fourth-grade girls everybody else was using regular three-speed bikes, not ten-speed like the one you used. So maybe you're just not such a great rider. Right, Ari?"

I didn't expect her to make me get into it, and I don't know what to say. So I just say, "Huh?" As if I didn't understand.

"I'm just saying that maybe the great Rhona Finkelstein isn't all that great," Jane says, and now practically the whole sixth grade is watching. And waiting for me to say something. But I don't. All I do is give a sort of sickly smile to both of them.

"Is that what *you* think, Ari?" Rhona says, and her eyes are all narrowed up and her face is about an inch away from mine and I don't know what to do. I really know what I should do but I think I'm still sort of scared of Rhona.

"You leave Ari alone," Jane orders, stepping between the two of us. "She doesn't have to say anything she doesn't want to."

I count to three, take a gigantic breath, and then I say, "Rhona?"

"Yeah?"

"Look, Rhona."

"Look what?"

If I don't do it now I never will and if I don't I'll lose the best friend I ever had. "Maybe if you practice you could get better at it. I know this boy, he lives in my building, and he couldn't ride so well so . . ."

"Are you saying I don't ride good?"

"Well . . ."

"Well what?"

"Well . . ." I look around and everybody is staring at me and Jane gives me a kind of secret smile and I say to Rhona, "You don't ride so good."

She looks shocked and really mad. But before she can do anything Jane jumps in and says, "Maybe we should choose someone else to represent us in the bike race."

And everybody starts nodding and saying, "Yeah," and "Maybe we should," and Rhona says, "That's not fair. I got chosen. It was a vote. You can't just change things like that."

And she's all upset. I never saw Rhona like that. Nobody else did either. You can tell from their faces they're really surprised.

"Well . . ." Jane has her hands on her hips and looks awful fierce. Rhona looks at her like Jane's the one in charge. I can't believe it. Rhona is actually taking orders from someone her own age. "I guess we can give her one last chance," says Jane, still staring Rhona down. "What do you think, Ari?"

"Well . . ." I love it all.

"Come on, Ari," Rhona says, and she's practically pleading. With *me*. Can you believe that?

"Ah, sure," I say, and I even give her a smile. I don't care so much if she rides in the race or not, but the great thing is that I just know she's never going to pick on me or push me around again. Absolutely not! And you know why?

Because I'm not going to let her!

That's the way Jane does it.

Jane's only my size and my age but people hardly ever push her around the way they do me . . . the way they *used* to do me. I've been watching her a lot, and I don't know exactly how she does it but I know *I'm* doing it a little now and it's working. I guess that sounds kind of nutty but maybe after I do it a few more times I'll know more about what it is.

Another funny thing. After I say it's okay for Rhona to be in the race, everybody else jumps in and says, "Well, okay," and "Sure thing," and all that. It's as though they were all waiting for me to decide. I'm not sure what that's all about yet either but maybe Jane knows. . . .

And then it gets even weirder because after I say sure to Rhona she thanks me. Actually uses the word "thanks" right in front of practically the whole class. That's the best thing that happened to me since I won the poetry contest in second grade. I got a plaque for that but this is lots better.

I hardly hear what the teacher is saying all morning because I can't stop thinking about what happened with Rhona. I go over it lots of times and now I have it to where I'm doing it all myself and I don't even need

Jane's help. After a while it's me helping Jane. This is the best morning I've had since the bike got stolen.

But it can't last because probably when I get home today the police will be there and then everybody will know the truth.

Later, just before lunch period, Jane and I are sitting alone in the classroom and I tell her how I was a little scared for a minute back there because nobody ever won over Rhona Finkelstein before.

"I think Rhona's just about the toughest person I ever knew in my whole life," I say.

"A lot of times bullies like that aren't nearly as tough as you think, Ari. Sometimes all you have to do is stand up to them and they fall apart."

"Except you don't know me. I'd probably fall apart first."

"Bet you wouldn't."

"You think so?"

"I know so."

Sometimes I could hug Jane. She makes me feel so good.

Now she gets serious-looking and says, "I even feel a little sorry for Rhona."

"How come?"

"Probably she doesn't even know how to be nice. Maybe nobody took the time to teach her."

"I bet her mother never did. She's hardly ever around."

"See what I mean?"

"Yeah. I guess so. . . ." But I keep thinking about how Rhona acted that morning in the park.

THIRTEEN

My mother comes up to school to drop off the present for Jane and I can tell she still doesn't know because she's still loving me a lot for what I did to save Eddie. The nicer they are to me the worse I feel. I act so peculiar that my mother wants to know if I'm okay. I tell her I am but she feels my head anyway, which makes me embarrassed because everybody's watching. I roll my eyes up like "Oh, my God!" but she does what she always does after she feels my forehead with her hand—she puts her lips to my head. It's really too much but you don't stop my mother when it comes to health. She probably should have been a doctor except she can't stand the sight of blood.

When my mother came Jane was in the girls' room so

we waited for her to come out because my mother wanted to meet her. I could tell right away that my mother liked Jane and she was very nice about wishing her a happy birthday and telling her that she has to come over to our house for dinner soon.

After my mother went home Jane said she thought my mother was very nice and a lot like her mother.

I'm getting excited about the party this afternoon. I always get so excited when I'm going to a party that I can't concentrate on anything else. What with the party and the showdown with Rhona I don't know what's going on at school at all. Luckily none of the teachers call on me for anything. Finally it's one-fifteen and we get dismissed. I feel very special because I'm the only one in our class invited to Jane's party.

A lot of the kids know it's her birthday and they say happy birthday and look like they wouldn't mind if she asked them to come with us. But she doesn't.

All we talk about on the way to her house is how we really won over Rhona and I tell her how everybody is so scared of Rhona and she says maybe if she had known that she would have been scared too. But I know she wouldn't have. She's so terrific. I love her. I really do.

A whole load of relatives and neighbors are at the house when we get there and they make a big fuss over Jane. It's lunch hour so some of the people who work, like her father and her uncle, can be there too. Her mother has this big table all filled with food—lasagna, salads, hot Italian bread, fried chicken—all kinds of delicious things, even the apple pie—and we all start eating right away. Her mother is a marvelous cook. I love it all. Her sisters are very nice to me and so is her brother Charles. It's a terrific day. If only I could get that bike back it would really be perfect.

After lunch we have to hurry to bring out the cake because some of the people have to get back to work. The cake looks beautiful. Jane's sister Jackie decorated it and it looks better than anything in a bakery. And it tastes much better, too.

When everyone finishes singing happy birthday and eating the cake Jane starts to open the presents.

I always worry that my present is going to be the worst. In fact, I hate it when people open the presents in front of everyone because I always think maybe mine is crummy. This time I'm absolutely wrong because Jane loves mine. My mother got her the album from the Broadway musical *Grease.* I have it and I play it all the time.

Jane comes over and gives me a kiss, and everybody says things like, "Oh, that's terrific," and "It's my favorite album," and all that, and I feel great.

There are a lot of presents and she makes a big fuss over all of them, which is very nice because then the people feel good about what they got her. Most of the things are really nice anyway. She gets two beautiful camisoles and some books and a sweater and some money from her aunt, and when she's finished opening all the little presents her father says, "And now for the grand finale! Da de de da!" and he throws out his arm toward the doorway and everybody turns and waits.

But nothing happens so everybody laughs and then

her father says, "Laura, where's the grand finale?"

"Hang on," Jane's mother calls from the other room. "It's coming."

"Charles"—her father motions to her brother—"go see if your mother needs help."

Charles heads into the other room, and Mr. Richardson explains to Jane that Charles is partly responsible for the present since he thought up the idea and helped pick it out.

Jane groans and everybody laughs.

I'm stuck behind Jane's Uncle Ben and all I can see is her mother and brother pushing something, and then Jane lets out the loudest squeal and starts jumping up and down and clapping her hands, and everybody says, "Oooh!" and "Aah!" and I squeeze in between her uncle and her grown-up cousin Effie and I finally get to see what all the excitement is about.

It's a bike. A beauty. In fact just like Liz's. It's a tenspeed Peugeot, and exactly the same color as Liz's. Jane is bursting she's so happy. "Oh, Mommy, Daddy!" she squeals. "Oh, I love it! Thank you, thank you!" And she gives them both big hugs and kisses.

I inch over to the bike because I'm beginning to get just the tiniest sick feeling in my stomach. The handlebars are what started my stomach sliding upside down. On most racing bikes they're almost facing the ground, making you lean way forward when you pedal. But Liz never cared about racing, so she made Eddie raise them. Jane's new bike has the handlebars in exactly the same position as Liz's. Another thing. Almost every bike you see has a black seat. But Liz hates black and loves beige, and that's the color seat she had on her bike. The same as Jane's!

Jane comes over to me, still all excited. "Don't you just love it?" she says. "And listen, you can borrow it any time you want."

"Thanks," I say. "It's really a beautiful bike." It's very hard for me to talk 'cause there's this big lump growing in the back of my throat. I stare hard at the bike. The bell's exactly where it is on Liz's bike. So are the two lights. I can feel tears beginning to bubble up in my eyes. There's no question about it and I've never felt more terrible in my whole life. It can't be but it is.

It's Liz's bike!

And then I stare even harder at her brother. She herself said that Charles was awful and mean and he *is* just about the same age as Bucky and . . . it's terrible to even think but maybe he's mixed up with those disgusting boys who stole the bike. They could be all part of a gang and Charles could even have been there that day without me seeing him because I was so busy trying to get the old man's hat back.

Now I'm really confused. It's all tumbling around in my brain like crazy—except for one thing. *That bike belongs to my sister. I just know it!*

FOURTEEN

I start quietly squeezing past people to the door. I can't stay here and watch any longer. I'm going to burst out crying any second and I have to get out. But when I get near the door Jane sees me and looks so surprised.

"Ari, where are you going?" she asks. "What's the matter?" But I'm already out the living-room door, and I don't stop. I just keep going as fast as I can, right out the front door and down the steps. And now I'm running and I don't even know which direction I'm going in because I'm crying so hard I can hardly see.

This is even worse than getting the bike stolen in the first place.

I keep running and crying and then I end up in the little park and there are hundreds of people there because of the bike race, but I don't care even if they're all looking. I just sit down on the first bench I can find and keep crying. The loud kind where everyone can hear you and you can't catch your breath.

"Hey, Ari!" It's Rhona and she's pushing through the crowd toward me. I hide my face as far into my hands as I can so she can't see. Still, I can't stop crying and I don't even want to.

"What's the matter, Ari?" she asks, sliding onto the bench next to me. "Did your new friend dump you?"

I just shake my head no. It's too hard to talk.

"Well, God, don't sit there sniffling. You look like such a baby."

Now I really let go.

"Hey, look . . ." she says, and I can tell I got her worried. I think she'll get up and get away fast but instead she moves a couple of inches closer to me and says, "Uh, Ari, is it something bad?"

I nod.

"Well, gee, in that case maybe I can do something to help you. Okay, so we're not such great friends any more—still, if you're in real trouble you know I've got some good contacts. I didn't tell you but my mother's cousin is the water commissioner. I could get in touch with him. What do you say? Want me to step in?"

I shake my head but I don't look up. My hands are all wet from my tears and my nose is running. I use the bottom of my T-shirt to wipe my face. And then Rhona just sits next to me and she doesn't ask me anything any more and that makes me feel a little better. I couldn't tell her now because it's even worse than before and before was pretty bad.

Just when I start to stop crying I hear Jane's voice calling me. I look up and—oh, God! She's come on Liz's bike! That makes me start all over again.

"Ari," she says, "what happened?"

Now I'm so miserable I'm crying out loud and I must sound like a little baby but I can't stop.

"Do you know what's wrong?" I hear Jane ask Rhona, and Rhona says, "Uh-uh."

I'm all hot and sweaty and wet from crying and I look up and start to wipe my face again with my shirt and then I see Liz and Eddie.

And Liz's bike is right out here in plain view! I'm terrified, but they don't see us because they're sitting on the grass facing the other way. Just seeing them scares the tears right out of me. I know if I keep making such a noisy fuss they'll definitely turn around and see the bike so I do the only thing I can think of to calm everything down. I take a huge deep breath and squeeze my lips into a giant smile, which I push right into both Rhona's and Jane's faces. They look really surprised.

"Gee!" is all Jane can say. Then she looks at Rhona and shrugs, and so does Rhona.

"Fooled ya, huh?" I say.

"Yeah, you sure did," Rhona says with a "what a nut" look on her face.

"Well," I say, lowering my voice a whole lot, "mayb we should go back to the party?"

"Are you sure you want to?" Jane asks me, reall confused.

"Well," I say, practically whispering, "let's just wal in that direction anyway." And I get up and start t

134

sort of move Jane and the bike in the direction away from my sister. But she's not moving.

"Ari," Jane says, "come on now, I know something's wrong. What's up?"

I make the smile even bigger. "Nothing, I swear. I really was pretending."

"Then why are you whispering?" Rhona says.

"Am I?" I whisper. "Maybe I've got strep throat."

"Hey, Ari," Jane says, and I squirm because it's surely loud enough for Liz to hear. I watch the back of Liz's head but she doesn't turn so she must not have heard. "What's the good of having a best friend if you can't trust her?"

"I'll tell you later," I say and then I see that was dumb because now Rhona is insulted. "Pardon me for living," Rhona says and picks up her jacket off the bench. She's steaming mad.

"I didn't mean it that way, Rhona—all I meant was that I couldn't talk about it now because I have to find out something else first. I was going to tell you later too. I swear."

"I'm probably going to be busy later," she says, sounding like the old Rhona.

"Oh, well, that's okay. It can wait."

"Oh, yeah? Well, uh, when later?"

You see? I didn't beg her. "Tonight. I'll call you."

"If I'm home," she says, and even though she still sounds annoyed, I can tell it's okay. I could never have acted like that before I met Jane. I really learned a lot just watching her.

While I'm talking, I sneak a peek at Liz and Eddie.

They're still sitting there, holding hands and telling each other secrets. Probably they don't even know anybody else is in the park. Lucky for me.

"Hold my bike for a second, please," Jane says, "I gotta tie my shoelace."

I wish we could get out of here, but I have to hold the bike. Jane does one shoe and then she decides the other one isn't right either so she takes the bow out and reties it. All the while I'm praying that my sister doesn't turn around. And lucky me, she doesn't.

"You could both come home with me," Jane says. "I know for sure there'll be some cake left."

"I can't," I say, "I was supposed to do something for my mother and"—now I see Liz starting to get up— "besides, I have to go home right now, and—well, goodbye. I'll see you later." And I shove the bike back to Jane and, still staring at Liz, who's busy brushing herself off, start to back away from Rhona and Jane.

"Yeah, well, see ya," I say, but I'm not looking at them. I've still got my eyes on Liz.

"Watch it, Ari!" Jane yells to me as I back into a big cement water fountain and my feet start to slide out from under me in the mud around it. At the last second I manage to grab onto the lip of the fountain and hang there with my backside an inch off the ground.

"Are you okay?" Jane stands her bike up and rushes over to me. Rhona comes too and they both pull my arms off the fountain and the rest of me away from the mud. All the while they're helping me I'm watching Liz. But she still doesn't see me. She's just standing there looking around at nothing. First she looks all the way over to the right, way past us, then slowly she starts to turn in our direction.

She keeps turning and turning and now she's practically looking right at us except she doesn't because that's when she spots the bike.

She stares for a few seconds and then she starts to walk toward it.

I can see her starting to get real excited as she comes closer and closer to it.

Now she's practically on top of it, and first thing she does is bend down and look under the seat, and then she jumps up, screaming, "Eddie! Eddie!" and he comes running over to her.

By now Jane and Rhona have turned around to see what I'm staring at and we all watch together like it's a scene on TV.

"That's your sister, isn't it?" Jane says, and I nod. "What's she doing with my bike?"

I can't speak, so I just shrug my shoulders and shake my head.

"Hi," Jane says, heading over to Liz and Eddie.

When Liz looks up she recognizes Jane and then she sees me.

"Ari! Look! I found it!" Liz is squealing and smiling and jumping up and down and hanging onto the handlebars tightly.

Jane looks at Liz, then at me, and her brown eyes get really big, and then she says in a really confused voice, "That's *my* bike."

I just shrug and try to slide behind Rhona.

Rhona's looking at everybody like they're crazy. She

knows something's wrong, but she can't figure out what.

"Can't be," Liz says, "it's mine, I know it. I can recognize my own bike when I see it."

"Uh-uh." Jane shakes her head. Then she puts one hand on the seat and the other on the rear fender like she's claiming it.

Now they're both holding the bike. This is terrible.

"Eddie," Liz says, starting to sound whiny, "tell her it's mine. You know it is."

"It sure looks like it. Same color seat and everything."

"I don't know what's going on here," Jane says, and her voice is beginning to tremble. "But I know I just got this bike from my parents today for my birthday. It's mine, and I'm taking it home right now!"

"Ari"—Liz pokes her head around Rhona to find me—"you know this is my bike. Tell her."

I come up to the bike and pretend to look it over. "It *looks* like yours," I say to Liz.

Jane gives me an awful look.

"Look, Jane," Liz says, sounding very grown-up, "my bike got stolen just a couple of days ago. . . ."

"Hey," Jane says, "I didn't take your bike. I told you I got this for my birthday."

"I didn't say *you* took it. I didn't mean that. I just meant that somebody stole this bike from me and then maybe whoever gave it to you . . ."

Now Jane is fuming. She steps up real close to Liz and with her hands on her hips says in a very angry voice, "My parents gave me that bike. Are you saying they stole it?"

"No," Liz says, "I didn't mean that. Absolutely not."

"Yeah, well, then, what *did* you mean?"

"Hey, wait a minute," Eddie cuts in. "All Liz meant was that maybe the people who stole the bike sold it to your folks."

Now Jane stomps over to Eddie and she practically hisses at him. "My parents don't buy bikes or anything else from crooks."

"Suppose they didn't know he was a crook," Eddie suggests.

Jane looks ice-cold at him. "You think they're dumb or something? My parents know what crooks look like better than you do. This is my bike, so please let go of it." Now for the first time I can see Jane is going to cry if it goes on any longer.

"Jane," my sister says in a very sweet voice, "I don't mean to insult you or your parents or anything like that. I think that maybe this could be my bike and we should find out because maybe somebody is tricking all of us. Would it be okay with you if I called your parents and asked them where they got the bike?"

"It's a free country—you can call whoever you want."

"Hey, really," Liz says, "don't get mad at me. I feel terrible about this whole thing too."

"Yeah, well, you shouldn't call people's parents thieves, you know."

"I'm sorry if you thought I did because I didn't mean to," Liz says, and I can tell she's really sorry.

With all this about whose bike it is everybody seems to have forgotten about me. We all walk over to the phone booth and I don't know who to walk with. I don't know whose side to be on. So far nobody's worried about *how* the bike got stolen. Rhona knows I had it in the park but so far she's kept still about it—I have the feeling she knows I'd be in big trouble if she told anyone. She can probably tell from my face. I glance at her and catch her staring at me. I look away fast.

Meanwhile Jane has phoned home and her mother answers.

"Mommy . . ." Her voice is shaking. "Ma . . . no, I'm okay . . . it's just that, well . . . no, I swear I'm not hurt . . . it's just that Ari's sister says it's her bike . . . no, *my* bike. She says it's hers because hers got stolen, and she says she recognizes hers as mine. And everybody's saying it *looks* like hers, even Ari."

We can't hear what her mother is saying, but we see Jane nod and look at Liz.

"Okay, Ma, I will," Jane says to her mother, and then to Liz, "My mother says they bought the bike yesterday, and they have the receipt. And she says the only thing to do is for all of us to go back to the bike shop together and get to the bottom of it."

"Okay," Liz says, "I'll call my parents too. What's the name of the bike shop?"

Jane asks her mother and she says, "Reinhardt's."

Gross. But I knew it had to be. Even so, I'm okay. Mr. Reinhardt barely looked at me, and besides, maybe nobody will care any more how the bike got stolen in the first place. I hope.

Liz calls Mommy at home and tells her the whole story, and she says she's going to tell Daddy at the office and they'll meet us at Reinhardt's in fifteen minutes.

We all troop down toward Eighth Street, past Delmonte's Luncheonette (I peek in to see if Bucky is there—he isn't) and on down to the East Village. It's like we're on opposite teams with Jane and Rhona on one side and Liz and Eddie on the other and me trying to stay someplace in the middle. Finally I can't stand it and I end up walking with Liz and Eddie. Well, she *is* my sister.

I wish the walk were longer, like at least four years, because it may be all over for me when we get to that store. Probably it'll come out how the bike got stolen in the first place and that's going to be horrendous. Liz will start screaming at me and even Eddie will hate me because of that terrible thing that almost happened to him.

And then the police are going to be angry because I lied to them, and they might even arrest me. If it's those same policemen from yesterday they surely will. Maybe that wouldn't be so bad. At least I wouldn't have to go home with Liz. She's never going to forgive me, I just know it. And of course nobody is ever going to believe me ever again. That makes me very unhappy—I mean, when you think that people are always going to think you're lying all the time. Just thinking about all that gives me a stomachache.

Jane will definitely despise me for always. She'll never be my friend again. Ever.

It's a strange walk, because no one is really saying anything much. Jane is very upset because I guess she must be worried about what will happen to her parents if they really did buy a stolen bike. Rhona is quiet too. I've never seen Rhona so quiet.

Do you know how scary it is to be involved in a crime

with the police? It's not like when you do something wrong at home; all they do is ground you or yell or something like that. But the police can send you to *jail*. And you have to *stay* there. Even if you apologize a million times, it still won't make any difference.

I didn't realize how hot it was. The sun is baking down, and it's all dry and dusty in the streets. Being so sweaty on account of the heat and being sweaty because you're scared really makes you a soggy mess. And my T-shirt is all grubby from when I was crying. Probably I look like a criminal already.

I think being a criminal must make you feel unhappy all the time. It's been the worst two days of my life already, and I've only just started doing crimes.

FIFTEEN

Just as we turn the corner near the bike shop a taxi pulls up and Jane's mother and father get out. Jane runs up to them, and even though I can't hear exactly what she's saying, both her parents look shocked and angry.

Everybody says fast hellos, and I can tell from the way Mr. and Mrs. Richardson are looking at me that they don't know whether or not they like me so much any more. Probably they're not thinking that at all. Probably they're thinking they hate me.

Jane is holding onto the bike, but Liz is standing pretty close to it. I'm busy wishing I was invisible. Mr. Richardson goes over to the bike and inspects it. "Well, that's certainly the bike I bought for you, Jane," he says to her. "Right in this store. Charles helped us pick it out." As he nods toward the store, I turn and see Mr. Reinhardt standing behind the cash register, watching us from the window. He doesn't look surprised or scared. He's just watching, not saying anything.

After a minute or two my parents turn the corner and spot us—and I can't believe it! A police car is pulling up and stopping right in front of us all. It's those two gross policemen who first came to my house. My heart starts pounding real hard. What are they doing here?

Liz introduces everyone, and Jane's parents and mine shake hands, and my mother says, "When Liz told me she'd found her bike I called the police to let them know. They said they wanted to come here to confirm the identification."

"Fine," says Mr. Richardson. "I'm glad to see the police here, but I'm afraid Liz is badly mistaken. It's not her bike. It's my daughter's."

"Well, if this is the item in question," says my father, walking around the bike and examining it very carefully, "then I'm afraid someone has sold you a stolen bike, Mr. Richardson. This is Liz's all right. I'd stake my life on it. The issue is, what do we do about it?"

By now the policemen have gotten out of their car and joined us. They don't even look at me. Everybody is getting introduced to the police and nobody at all is looking at me, not even Rhona who's staring bug-eyed in fascination at the policemen, and I'm the *cause* of all the trouble. How much longer is it going to be before they all find out?

Except for Eddie who's sort of hanging back, staying as far away from the policemen as he can, everyone else is just standing around and talking like nothing was wrong. It's really weird. If the policemen weren't there, you'd think it was just a couple of families, probably next-door neighbors or something, who met on the street while they were out for a walk and are just talking about nothing much special. Jane's parents and mine are about the same age and they're even dressed alike—our mothers are in jeans and T-shirts and our fathers are in gray business suits. But the policemen *are* there—all because of me—and the people passing on the street are staring at us, and they all know something must be wrong. It's getting hotter and I'm sweating more and more. I just wish I could go home.

I force myself to listen to what they're saying, and Officer Fitzroy is telling everyone, "Well, I think the first thing we do is pop in on old Otto here," and he nods toward Reinhardt's. "Otto's an old friend of ours, used to run a used-car lot over on West Street—stolen cars had a funny way of ending up on old Otto's lot with a different coat of paint on them. We had him down at the station—what was it, Bill—five or six times?—before he went out of business."

"Something like that," says Officer Jones. Gee, his name is Bill. That's a nice friendly name for such a mean cop.

"And now he's in bikes," Officer Fitzroy says, "and lately there's suddenly a whole rash of bike thefts. We've been watching old Otto, but he's no dope. He's tricky. Let's see if he's got any tricks up his sleeve now."

And everybody, even Eddie, turns and goes into Reinhardt's bike shop.

I make sure I'm the last one in. I'm not as afraid as I was on Saturday. With Daddy here and the policemen and everyone, Mr. Reinhardt's not going to hit me or yell at me. What makes me a little scared, though, is that he's sure to recognize me and maybe ask questions and that would lead to other questions and I don't think I can hold out much longer. I whisper to no one in particular, "Gee, it's hot," and I put my hair tight in a pony tail with a rubber band I always carry, as though I'm trying to make myself cooler. Actually what I'm really doing is trying to disguise myself. I don't think it will work but it's worth trying. I wish I had a pair of sunglasses to put on.

"Well, Otto," says Officer Jones, poking around the bikes in the store and looking at some of the price tags. "I see you got plenty of bikes here. Business must be pretty good."

"What are you guys doing here, Jones?" Mr. Reinhardt asks in a real grumpy voice. "What's going on here?"

"Why does anything have to be going on, Otto?" Officer Fitzroy says. "What makes you think this isn't just a friendly little visit? What's the matter, got something on your conscience?"

Oh, boy, this is real detective work, like when they have a suspect on a TV show and all the cops are grilling him. It's so exciting I forget I'm the criminal everyone's really after.

"You guys never come on a friendly visit," says Reinhardt to the policemen. "These people got a beef against me or something?"

Mr. Richardson speaks up. "Not really, Mr. Reinhardt," he says. "My wife and I bought this bicycle from you yesterday—for my daughter's birthday today. My son picked it out. I'm sure you remember."

"Right," says Mr. Reinhardt.

Mr. Richardson takes out the receipt. "And here's the receipt you gave me. This *is* the bike, isn't it? There's no mistake about that."

"That's the bike," says Mr. Reinhardt, hardly looking at it. "Two hundred and thirty bucks."

Liz pipes up, "That's my bike. Tell them, Eddie."

"I'd know that bike anywhere. I fixed the seat myself," he says, and then he moves up real close to Liz like he's going to protect her. I can't understand how he could like her so much.

Mr. Reinhardt stares at her a minute, then looks around at the policemen and finally at me. Then like a sledgehammer hitting me on the head, he says right at me, "Is that your sister?"

Everyone turns to look at me. I could die. I gulp a couple of times and say, "Yeah."

"Hey, what's going on here?" Liz demands. She frowns at me. "How come he knows that?" she asks me.

"She was in here Saturday, bawling all over the place, saying her sister's bike was stolen," Mr. Reinhardt says. He looks at Officer Fitzroy. "What is this, the children's hour, Fitz? Come on, get these people out of here. I'm busy."

"Just a moment, Mr. Reinhardt," my mother says.

"There's a very serious question of ownership here, and we insist on straightening it out."

He's about to say something, but Liz has been looking hard at me and suddenly snaps at me, "What were you doing here?"

The way she says it scares me. "I was trying to find your bike," I say.

"I don't mean that. I mean why are you so busy concerning yourself about *my* stolen bike. You'd never lift a finger for me if you didn't have to, so why the sudden big interest in my bike?"

I look at my mother and father for help. But I guess they're curious, too.

"I don't know," I say. "I just wanted to help."

"I'm sure you did," my father says, "but why did you come to this particular bike store?"

I don't know what to say, so I just shrug.

Now my mother looks at me very strangely. "Daddy's right," she says. "This is at least a fifteen-minute walk from our house. What were you doing in this neighborhood anyway?"

"Ma, she knows something and she's not saying."

"You leave me alone!" I practically shout at Liz. She still scares me, but I don't care.

"Will you get this circus out of here!" Mr. Reinhardt says to the policemen.

"Keep your shirt on, Otto," Officer Fitzroy replies. "Nobody's going anywhere till we get a few things straightened out here."

Liz is glaring at me. "I'd like to know how that bike got stolen," she says, "that's what I'd like to know."

Now suddenly Rhona gets into it. "I think I'm the cause of it all," she says quietly. "I didn't know it was going to end up with the police and everybody arguing all over the place." She looks at me. "And I didn't really mean to cause so much trouble for Ari. She's kind of a good friend, and besides, I've never seen anyone cry so much."

Oh, boy, why did she have to get to be such a good friend all of a sudden! Now everything's going to come out. It's starting and I can't stop it. I stare down hard at my toes and keep looking. I can feel everybody staring at me. It gets really quiet. I think they're waiting for me to say something, but I don't. Finally I peek up and Liz is looking at my parents and then she turns to me, then Rhona.

"What have you got to do with any of this?" she asks Rhona. She's really puzzled.

"Well, I guess it started when you agreed to lend me the bike. I didn't believe Ari when she said some kids stole it. But now I know they really did."

"Wait a minute," Liz says. "What do you mean—when I agreed to lend you the bike? I never lent you my bike."

"Well, Ari said she was going to borrow the bike from you so I could use it in the school race. Isn't that what you told me, Ari?"

Jane is watching me closely. So are her parents. And Eddie too. Even the policemen are waiting for me to answer. It seems everybody's more interested in me than they are in catching the real thief, that rat Bucky.

Liz spins on me. "Well, you little brat," she snaps.

"You're the one who took my bike. I'll kill you!"

And she makes a leap for me, but my father steps in front. "Daddy," Liz squeals, "she took my bike!"

I'm so afraid of what's going to happen that I start to cry. And now I can't believe it! Rhona's face starts to get all red and her freckles turn into blotches and she begins to cry too, and she says, "Wait, d-d-don't be angry with Ari. It really is all my fault." She takes this big bandana that looks like a kitchen towel out of her pocket and blows her nose. "I'm always doing stupid things like that," she goes on. "I practically bullied Ari into getting me Liz's bike—and now I feel awful."

"Now try to stop crying, dear," my mother says to her, and smooths Rhona's hair with her hand. "You too, Ari," she adds.

But Rhona can't stop talking. "I'm always so afraid nobody's going to like me that I try to *make* them like me—it's like I'm always telling everyone, 'You better like me or else!' It's so stupid. God, I wish I had a sister so I could have a best friend right in my own family!"

"Hah!" says Liz. "Ari's no best friend of mine. And the idea of my lending her my bike is crazy—no way!"

"Why not?" That's Jane asking the question.

"Now you stay out of it," Mrs. Richardson tells Jane. "This has nothing to do with our problem and we're not getting any closer to a solution. It's very clear that you and Liz Jacobs both own the bike and something's got to be done about it."

I'd practically forgotten that's what we're all here for. All I can do is whimper and sob and try not to say anything because if I do it'll be the wrong thing and I'll be sorry for the rest of my life, even though I don't think I can be any sorrier than I am now. My mommy gives me a tissue and I blow into it. It sounds like a goose honking, and besides everything else, now I'm embarrassed, too.

"But, Ma," Jane says, and she's actually looking at Liz, "why shouldn't sisters lend things sometimes? If Jackie or Regina wanted to borrow my bike for a special reason, I'd lend it."

"Yes," my mother says, talking to Liz. "Just why is it you can't lend your own sister your bike?" She sounds a little bit angry, and I look at Liz to see what she's going to say.

"Because," says Liz, "she's a pest. And . . . and . . ."

Oh, my gosh, I think Liz is going to bawl now, too.

". . . and you're always nicer to Ari than you are to me, and it's so unfair how you favor her just 'cause she's the youngest and—" But she can't go on because, sure enough, here come the tears. This whole place is starting to look like somebody died.

"Well, that is simply not so," says my mother to Liz. "I'm surprised to hear you say that. You know I love you both equally. We'll discuss this further when we get home, but I want you to know I don't like to see that kind of selfishness and I won't have it. If Ari hadn't been afraid to ask for the bike, maybe none of this would have happened. And to tell you the truth, I'm really not quite sure just what did happen. Arianne, I think you have a lot of explaining to do."

And so I do. I tell them the whole story with everything in it. I mean the whole truth about Rhona and sneaking the bike for the race and the old man in the park and Bucky and the other kid and even about Bucky's grandmother and the boy in the bowling alley saying how Bucky hangs out at Reinhardt's a lot.

When I mention Mr. Reinhardt, Officer Jones walks over to the door and closes it. "Well, well, Otto," he says, "ain't that a coincidence."

"Listen, Jonesy," Mr. Reinhardt says to the officer. "Book me or get out of here and take your friends with you. You got nothing on me, nothing. I sold that bike to these people here yesterday and they have the receipt. I don't know nothing about this other kid's bike. You can't prove a thing against me, and if you don't leave right now I'll have you up in front of the commissioner for harassment." He turns to my father. "If you're accusing me of selling a stolen bike, make your complaint and I'll have my lawyer on your back so fast you'll see stars. I'll sue you for every penny you have."

His face is all red and he's breathing hard. There doesn't seem to be anything anybody can do. My parents and the Richardsons just stand there. They both bought the same bike but they don't know who gets to keep it. You just don't hand over a very expensive bike like that to somebody else. It's such a horrible problem and nobody can solve it and it's all my fault. The two policemen are starting to ease us all out of the store and just when they get to the doorway I look out and practically in front of the store heading right for the door is that gross awful kid.

The stealer.

That rotten Bucky!

SIXTEEN

He takes one look at me and swings around and starts running. I push right past the policemen's legs and start flying after him as fast as I can.

Neither of us can go so fast because the street is too crowded with people. He keeps weaving in and out, trying not to bump into them, and I'm right there behind him and I'm going to grab him if it's the last thing I do because I'm so angry all I care about is catching that rotten Bucky and punching his head in.

He practically trips over a baby in a stroller and it gives me a chance to close the gap and I do and I'm not even out of breath yet.

He looks around to see if I'm still there and practically runs smack into a big fat lady who starts screaming at him. Then her husband or somebody grabs Bucky's arm and now's my chance to get him.

I'm almost right up to him when he yanks his arm free and swings around behind another lady and then for a second he's out of sight and then he pops up again just a couple of feet away from me. His shirt's flying straight out the back close enough so that I can make a grab for it and I almost get it but it slips through my fingers.

We're turning the corner now and there aren't so many people and he's going faster. I've got to get him now or he'll get away. We hit another patch of people in front of the subway and he slows down to get past them and I'm almost up to him again and this may be my last chance so I dive as hard as I can, just like I'm going into the water.

I go flying right for his legs and I land on them. I grab on with all my might and I can feel him toppling over, and then he's on the ground and I am too but I still have him. I clench my teeth and hang on. I feel him trying to push me off with his feet but I wrap my arms around tighter and I'm never going to let go. Ever!

Now he swings up to a sitting position, and he's punching me on the head and cursing me, and it hurts like crazy. I can't get out of the way unless I let go of his legs. First I try to hang on with one arm but he pushes me off with his foot, and now I have to let go both his legs and I try to grab his arm but I can't hold him down because he's too strong for me. Now he shoves me out of the way and starts to get up when suddenly—*boom!* Some giant thing lands smack on his chest and slams him back down with an awful thud.

Somebody's foot is in my face. I slide out of the way so I can get up and look, and there she is—supergiant! My own second best friend, Rhona Finkelstein, and, boy, is she giving it to Bucky! She's got him flat on the ground with her knees pinning his arms down and one hand holding his head by his hair and the other shoving his chin back so far he can't move at all.

Especially since Jane is sitting on his legs.

I didn't even see either one of them behind me, but now we've got Bucky, all three of us, and he's done for. Absolutely finished. In fact, his face is so red and scared-looking I think he's going to cry, which I would love to see because everything, this whole horrible mess, is all his fault.

"You took my bike," I scream right into his sweaty face, "you stinking rotten rat!"

"I did not!" he says.

"You did too! You liar!"

"Did not."

"You tell that to the police," Jane says.

"Yeah," Rhona says, "we're taking you back to the police."

"Hey, no, please don't do that," Bucky says, and now he really is crying. "It wasn't my fault. He made us do it."

"Who did?" I ask him.

"Reinhardt. The guy who owns the bike store."

All three of us gawk at each other. "Oh, boy," Jane says.

Rhona squints her eyes real suspicious-like and leans

down about an inch away from Bucky's face. "How can anybody make you steal anything if you don't want to?"

"He did!" Bucky yelps. "I swear it!"

"Yeah? How?"

"Let me up and I'll tell you."

"No way," Rhona says, pushing Bucky's head back farther. "I want to know *now*."

"Okay, okay . . . only let go my hair."

Rhona lets up a little on his hair, and he starts to tell us the story of how he stole the bike. Only now he's really crying hard, and Rhona lets go of him so he can wipe his eyes.

"One time Reinhardt caught us, me and my friend, Georgie Harris," he says. "We were fooling around and we stole the lights off some of his bikes, and he got us, and he knew our names and he was going to call the police and have us arrested unless we did what he said. First he wanted us to do little stuff, like snitching parts like horns or lights and that kind of thing, and then he'd pay us. I don't know—maybe a dollar or two. Then last week he said we had to swipe whole bikes. We told him we didn't want to, but he said if we didn't do it he'd turn us in to the cops, and he even had a witness because there's this guy here who fixes the bikes and he was going to say we stole bikes and that he saw us do it. So that's how come we stole your bike." The last part he says to me.

"You're going to tell that to the police," Rhona says, "and right now."

Now Bucky's crying again. "I can't . . . Reinhardt'll send me to jail."

"You let us take care of Mr. Reinhardt." A voice comes from behind us. It's Officers Fitzroy and Jones, and they're with my parents and Jane's parents.

Mr. Richardson gives Jane a hand up, and then Rhona gets off Bucky and he gets up. He sort of turns away so we can't see him wiping his eyes. Now he's really freaking out. He knows everybody heard what he said about stealing the bike, especially the police.

He looks at them and asks in this little voice, "Am I under arrest?"

"Maybe," says Officer Jones. "Depends. You wait right there a minute and don't move."

The two policemen walk off a few steps and talk in low voices. I wish I could hear what they're saying, but they're practically whispering. Once or twice they look at Bucky. Finally they come back.

"Would you be willing to tell a court that Reinhardt coerced you into stealing that bike?" Officer Fitzroy asks Bucky.

"Coerced?"

"Threatened you."

Bucky looks uneasy. "You mean I'd have to go to court?"

"Maybe, maybe not," says Officer Jones. "But if we can count on you as a witness we can all go back to Otto's and have a little chat with him. I got a feeling that nice big kindhearted Otto is going to help us straighten this whole mess up."

We all march back to Mr. Reinhardt's. The rest of us wait outside while the two policemen and Bucky go inside. They close the door, and we can't hear what they're saying, but we can see them, and Mr. Reinhardt looks like he's ranting and raving and shaking his head. I can see him yelling at Bucky, and after a while Bucky kind of picks his head up and starts yelling back at Mr. Reinhardt. Then Officer Fitzroy puts his hand on Mr. Reinhardt's arm and starts to move him toward the door. I can see Mr. Reinhardt saying the word "wait." There's some more conversation and then Mr. Reinhardt looks like he's breathing out a big sigh and nods.

Officer Jones walks to the door and motions us inside. "Well," he says, "it looks like the case of the stolen bike may be over. Tell these nice people what you're going to do, Otto."

Mr. Reinhardt grinds his teeth, but he doesn't say anything.

"Tell them, Otto." This time Officer Jones's voice is real sharp.

"Okay, okay." Mr. Reinhardt looks around his shop at the different bikes and then says to Mr. Richardson, "I'm not admitting anything, understand, but you paid for a new Peugeot and you deserve one. What do you think of that green ten-speeder over there?"

"I don't know. I suppose it looks okay to me," Mr. Richardson says. "What about you, Jane?"

Jane goes over to the bike and checks it out. It's exactly the same as Liz's, same make and all, only it's green. "Looks good to me, Daddy," Jane says, "and I even love the color."

"It's yours, honey," says that disgusting Reinhardt.

"Can I, Daddy?" Jane asks.

"What about it, Officer Fitzroy?" Mr. Richardson asks the policeman.

"And this bike goes back to the Jacobs?" Officer Fitzroy says to Reinhardt.

"Of course," he says. "It's the little girl's, isn't it?"

"Oh, boy," Liz says, "he's too much."

But both Jane and Liz are so happy with their bikes that they both smile at one another and then start laughing.

"Well, that would seem to solve things nicely, wouldn't you say?" Mr. Richardson asks my father.

"Pretty neat," my father says, and they shake hands. "We'll have to rehash this some night over dinner. How about it?"

"Just give us a call any time," says Mr. Richardson. "We'd be delighted."

"Just to keep the record straight," says Officer Fitzroy. "Bucky has—uh—volunteered to work a couple of afternoons a week at the PAL. Him and his buddy, the Harris kid, haven't you, Bucky?" Bucky shrugs and nods. "And we could use some older folks, too, come to think of it," Officer Jones says to Mr. Reinhardt, "particularly respected businessmen like yourself. What about it, Otto?"

"Well, I'm a pretty busy man. . . ."

"Otto . . ."

"But not too busy if the children need me." He's grinding his teeth again.

"So," says Officer Fitzroy. "There's been no crime that I know of in this case." He looks directly at me. "No crime at all, Ari, do you understand?"

All of a sudden I could hug him.

As we all leave the store, Liz is so excited about getting her bike back that she can't stop smiling at everybody, even once accidentally at me. And Eddie is smiling and Jane, too, because she was really worried, not just about losing her bike but about what would happen to her parents for buying something that was stolen. I'm glad I was wrong about her brother. So far, it's all turning out pretty good even with all the parents. They're all being so friendly it's like they've known each other for years. And Rhona and Jane are like they're best friends too, which I don't like a whole lot because Jane is really mostly my friend—at least she was starting to be before all this happened.

"Do you have time to make the race?" Jane asks Rhona.

"It doesn't make any difference," she says. "I don't have a bike anyway."

"Sure you do."

"Yeah, how?"

"I'll lend you mine."

"That's super!" Rhona says, and asks my dad what time it is.

It turns out that if we all really move fast maybe she can make the race. Rhona gets on Jane's bike and Liz gets on hers and they head for the park. The rest of us jump into one of those big checkered cabs, and you should see the driver's face when all seven of us pile in, but my mother tells him about the race and he's a nice man and it's just a few blocks, so he takes us to the entrance of the park where they have the starting line. We beat Rhona and Liz there, but they're only a couple of minutes behind us. Rhona gets up to the starting line, and we all cheer like crazy, and then some other kids from my school are there, and they go nuts when they see Rhona.

The race is ten times around the outside lane of the little park. There are probably about twenty-five kids in the race. Rhona looks fabulous, and she's got the nicest, newest bike of anybody.

"On your mark. Get set. Go!" And the whole pack of them zooms off. Rhona's looking great and Jane grabs my hand and starts jumping up and down shouting and I do too and it's terrific because we really are going to be best friends after all.

SEVENTEEN

Rhona rode the race on Jane's bike and came in fourteenth, but it didn't matter so much anyway because everything turned out so terrific, what with getting the bikes back and all the parents ending up feeling good and Jane and me being best friends again.

Afterwards we all stuck around for a while, taking turns riding the bikes, even the parents. Jane let me ride hers because for sure Liz wasn't going to forgive me that quick, and besides, she never lends anyway.

But that's okay because by the time we left to go home Jane and I had made plans for a bunch of sleepovers and we even let Rhona in for some, and our parents said fine and that's all that matters anyway.

When we got to our house, all of us, even Eddie, went into the kitchen and sat around the table, and my father started to talk about the whole thing and he said that even though everything turned out okay, what I had done was very bad.

"You know that, don't you?" my mother asked.

"I know, Mommy, and I'm really sorry. I swear to God and hope to die that I'll never do anything like that again in my whole life." And I said how these were the grossest three days in my whole life. "I felt so unhappy I couldn't stop thinking about it, and all I did was cry."

"What's so different about that?" Liz said, and I knew she was just being mean because she was still kind of angry.

"I'm really sorry, Liz," I told her, "and I promise I'll never ever borrow anything of yours without asking."

And then I said how sorry I was to Eddie, and he was so nice about it. He said that it was mostly that one cop. "He just didn't like Puerto Ricans, but I know you didn't mean that to happen, and you would have said something if it got any worse."

"I swear I wouldn't've let them take you. I swear it!"

"I know," and then he said how we should all forget it because it was really worse for me than anyone else.

"Eddie's right," my mother said. "I'd rather just plain lose something than be responsible for someone else's loss. That's an awful burden."

Everybody agreed with my mother, even Liz. "That's the worst," she said. "I mean to have to lie and cover up and know it's all your fault. I would just hate that."

"You should have confided in us, Arianne," my father said, and then my mother said that maybe they could have helped.

"I was afraid you would be angry."

"Well, we would have been," she said, "but still we'd have helped you, and believe me, our anger wouldn't have been half as bad as what you suffered with all the lies and sneaking around. That's the most terrible feeling of all."

Then my father said there was one thing he *was* pretty proud about and my mother said she knew what he was referring to and she agreed but I couldn't imagine what they were talking about.

"That was very courageous of you, Ari," my father said.

"What do you mean, Daddy?" I really couldn't think of what terrific thing I did.

"Coming to the aid of that old man. Those boys were pretty big and tough for a girl your size."

"I should say," my mother said, and then she hugged me to her. "You're a very brave young lady and we're proud of you."

"I just don't like to see anybody get picked on like that. I think it's mean and unfair," I said, and then Liz said how I was probably an expert on what it's like to get picked on, and I said, "Yeah. You bet," and everybody laughed and I was beginning to feel much better when Neddy walked in.

"Hey," he said, "what did I miss?"

"Nothing," Liz said, and that was practically the nicest thing she ever did for me since the time she made Neddy stop cutting my doll's foot off.

All that happened three days ago and everything is a

whole lot different now. At least it is for me. Since then and especially since I began to be good friends with Jane I've really changed.

I think Neddy can tell too, because lately he's not trying to tease me so much, and for the last three nights, even though he picked on me a lot at dinner I didn't cry once. I know everybody was expecting me to but I fooled them all.

Last night was the best.

"Well, Ari," he started in that super nice phony voice he uses for teasing, "borrowed any bikes lately?"

I didn't say a word, didn't even look up, just kept eating.

But my mother jumped in with her warning voice. "Neddy, watch—"

"Just asking, Ma." Then he got right back to me. "Say, I've been missing my new Bee Gees record. You didn't happen to accidentally lend it to that nine-foot geek friend of yours, huh?"

I turned to my mother. "Mommy . . ."

"I know, honey. *Neddy!* That's enough."

". . . could I have the last piece of corn?" I asked, like Neddy wasn't even there.

Everybody stopped eating and stared at me. Even Neddy.

"It's okay with me if someone else wants it," I said.

"No, no, no," my father said quickly. "You have it."

"Absolutely," my mother agreed instantly.

"Neddy," my father said, "pass Ari that piece of corn."

Then Neddy got real uptight, "Hey, maybe I want it."

"Right this minute!" My father used the voice that means business, and Neddy hopped to it.

I looked straight at Neddy, gave him a really sweet gooey smile, and snapped the corn right out of his hand.

I figured out a way to do it, and I'm never going to tell anyone except Jane. It's really terrific, and it works. What I do is as soon as Neddy begins to tease me, I start to say this poem to myself we learned in school last year. It's called "The Raven," and it's by Edgar Allan Poe, and it's got a lot of really good rhymes in it like, "Once upon a midnight dreary, while I pondered weak and weary," and on and on like that. You can say it very fast if you don't have to think about what it means. All I do is rattle it off to myself fast as I can like it's a race to see how many times I can say it before Neddy gives up teasing me. The first couple of nights I had to say it right to the end two times, but last night at dinner I barely got through the first half. It's definitely working, and he can't tell how I'm doing it. Nobody can, not even my parents, and they're really smart. It makes a big difference in the way the food tastes too. It's much better without tears all over everything.

Probably I'm not going to be like Jane overnight. I mean she's so strong about everything, and she feels so good inside herself. Still, I have a way that makes it look like you can't push me around so much any more. It's like I'm not a baby the way I used to be.

And I'm even trying to be like Jane about the hand-me-downs too. Now that I got Neddy where he can't push me around so much any more I feel sort of excited about myself, like I'm pretty smart. And you know what? Even the hand-me-downs don't seem so bad. I'm looking at them more like Jane says, kind of like extra bonus things, and it doesn't make any difference who had them because once they're mine, they're all mine.

Then there's one thing I did that's just like what Jane did with her bunk bed, only it's with a kimono instead. Liz was cleaning out her drawers, and she put a lot of old stuff in some shopping bags and said that if I went down and got her some polish remover I could go through them and keep anything I wanted. Most everything was a mess, really rags except for this old kimono that Liz used to practically live in. (I always loved it.) Some of the seams were open and the belt was missing, but my mother ran the whole thing up on the machine, and she even made me a skinny belt out of some of the extra inside material, and when she finished it looked like new. I can't wait to wear it.

Today the minute I get home from school I change into my kimono. I've been listening outside Liz's door for her to get off the phone so I can show it to her.

She's on the phone with Eddie, and it's so boring. He never seems so funny when he's here, but on the phone he must be the best comedian in the world because all she does is this dumb giggle for practically the whole conversation. Finally she's starting to say good-bye, which takes forever. Isn't that ridiculous to say good-bye for a whole ten minutes?

Hooray, she's off. I knock on her door.

"What?" she says, pretty nice in case it's my parents.

"Could I come in?"

"What do you want? I'm busy." In her regular voice.

"I just wanted to show you something."

There's a long silence and then she says, "Okay, come in, but make it fast."

I push the door open and I can't wait because I know she's going to be really surprised.

"Remember this?" I say, turning around like I'm a model.

"Where'd you find the belt?" she wants to know.

"I didn't. Mommy made me a new one, and she fixed all the seams too."

She doesn't even say another word. She just jumps up and races out of the room.

"Mom! Ma!" I hear her shouting down the hall.

I can tell there's going to be trouble, so I shoot right after her. My mother is making meatballs in the kitchen. She's standing at the stove, rolling little balls and dropping them into a big pot of boiling sauce. Meatballs and spaghetti is my second favorite dinner in the whole world. I don't know whether I should eat in my kimono because the food's really sloppy and drippy and I don't want to get any stains on it.

"Ma . . ." Liz is starting to whine. "How come you fixed the kimono for Ari?"

"Because she asked me to."

"That's no fair. I wouldn't have given her my favorite robe if I thought it could be fixed." Then she turns to me and in a fairly nice voice she says, "Ari, I've changed my mind."

Oh, no! My beautiful robe. I don't say anything. I just

look at my mother. She's still rolling meatballs.

"Maaa . . ." Liz is really upset. "I want my robe back."

Now my mother stops rolling and wipes her hands on some paper toweling. "I don't know, Elizabeth."

"You know it's my robe, Mom. You were the one who gave it to me."

"Then why did you give it to Ari?"

"I didn't give it to her."

"You did too," I say.

"I did not. I threw it in the garbage and then I told you you could go through the bags and take what you want. Boy, you are really ungrateful."

Now my mother sits down on the stool and says very calmly to Liz, "Sounds to me like you gave the robe up and Ari claimed it and now it's hers."

"It's mine and I want it back!" Elizabeth sounds just like a baby.

I don't say anything. I'm just holding my breath and looking hard at my mother.

"Well, Ari," my mother says, "I think it's up to you."

Liz comes up to me and her face starts to change while I'm watching. It's like Neddy does, except the opposite. Liz's face goes from real scary angry to nothing to nice and then all the way to marshmallow-syrup sweet.

"Ari," she says, leaning so close I almost think she's going to kiss me, "you know how I love that robe."

I nod my head yes.

"And how I wear it all the time."

Uh-uh . . .

"I would really like it back."

I look back at my mother, but she shakes her head and says, "I can't get involved in this. You girls will have to work it out yourselves."

Me against Liz! Oh, no . . .

The syrup starts oozing out again. Liz says, "I could give you that candleholder you like or my silver comb . . ."

I really like that comb. But I like the robe better.

"Uh-uh," I say.

"Pretty please . . ." I can't believe Liz really said that to me.

I never got a chance to say no to Liz about anything ever before. Even though she's being really nice, still I'm scared.

I shake my head no again and the sweet smile on her face starts to twist into a mean cat look and her top lip almost looks like it has whiskers and I look around for my mother but she's got her back to us and she's rolling the meatballs again. I feel like I'm all alone and Elizabeth is an army.

"You better give me that robe back or you'll be sorry."

I look around again at my mother but it's as though she's not there.

Just like always, lumps are growing in my throat and tears are starting in my eyes.

"I'll never do anything for you again, ever. Unless you give me back *my* robe."

Onceuponamidnightdreary. . . .

"Well?"

. . . whileIponderedweakandweary . . . The tears are shrinking and I can swallow better, overmanyaquaintandcuriousvolumeofforgottenlore . . .

"I'm warning you . . ."

whileInoddednearlynappingsuddenlytherecameatapping . . .

"GIVE ME MY ROBE THIS MINUTE!"

"No."

That was me. It was very soft so I don't know if she heard me.

"You brat! You stink!"

She heard me.

"I hate you!" she screams and runs out of the room.

I don't move. Maybe I'll never move. It's quiet in the kitchen except for the sound of bubbling sauce. Somewhere in the back of the house Liz is carrying on about how I can never borrow anything of hers or use anything or talk to her or anything. Now my mother turns around and looks at me and there's the tiniest smile at the corner of her mouth for a second, and then she turns back to the meatballs.

I wonder how long I can stay in the kitchen.

Suddenly it gets very quiet in the back of the house.

Now I hear Liz's footsteps coming back into the kitchen and I feel like running or hiding or anything. My heart is pounding so hard it's making my ears ring.

I hear Liz clunk down the back hall, through the dining room and the pantry, and then she's here. She's furious and I practically expect to see steam coming out of her head.

"Ari . . ." I jump. Her voice is so mean she sounds

like a witch. I don't even want the horrible robe any more.

"...do you think...uh...maybe I could borrow it sometime?"

"Huh?" I can't believe what I just heard.

"Do you think I could borrow my robe sometimes?"

I won. I won over the whole Elizabeth army. All by myself. I guess this is my big chance to pay Elizabeth back for all the awful things she's always doing to me. I could do just what she would do. It's easy, you know. All you have to do is get up real close to the other person and look them straight in the face and scream, "No! Never! You can never borrow my robe ever! Not for as long as you live! Creep! NEVER!!!!!!!!!" Most of the time that's enough to hurt the other person a whole lot. And I ought to know.

But I'm not going to do that. Remember how I said I would never treat her the way she treats me? Well, I'm not going to. Mostly because I hate to be nasty like that. I don't like the way it makes me feel inside. Right this minute I'm so happy that I'm smiling all over the place and it's very hard to be mean when you're feeling so good. So I say to Liz in a very nice voice, "Maybe. Yeah, I think so," and I look at her and I'm still smiling.

"Well," Liz says, and she begins to smile a little herself, "I guess that'll be okay."

Wait till I tell Jane.